TRIED AND TRUE

IN DOG TOWN

BY SANDY RIDEOUT

Tried and True in Dog Town

Copyright © 2018 Sandy Rideout

ISBN 978-1-9994313-8-9 eBook
ISBN 978-1-9994313-9-6 Book
ASIN B07GY3NDRT Kindle
ASIN 1999431391 Paperback

Publisher: Sandy Rideout
www.sandyrideout.com
Cover designer: Elizabeth Mackey
Editor: Serena Clarke
1810011717

Available on Kindle and other online stores

For Yvonne...

Whose love for Dexter inspired my passion for all things dog.

TRIED AND TRUE

She's the new judge in Dog Court. Someone is out to reveal her four-legged secret. Can she save her dog, her job and her marriage before it's too late?

Marti Forrester hates saying no, especially to the Mayor of Dorset Hills. When he appoints her to preside over Dog Court, she steps up—even though Hank, her loveable mutt, is the poster dog for poor training. Hank's misdeeds nibbled away at her marriage until husband Oliver took a break…and the dog.

Now Hank is back and she's scrambling to cover his dirty tracks to avoid a scandal. Can she do some good for the bad dogs of Dog Town despite this canine conflict of interest?

When someone threatens to expose Marti and imperil Hank, she digs deep into the secrets of Dog Town's old guard. The politics turn deadly, giving her one chance to save her beloved pooch and her floundering marriage before she loses them forever.

Tried and True in Dog Town is part of the "Dog Town" series of romantic comedies. If you like charming small-town capers with lots of heart and a little mystery, you'll love Sandy Rideout's novels.

Sink your teeth into this Dog Town confection today!

You can read the Dog Town series in any order. If you want to travel the seasons with the residents of Dorset Hills, however, here is the list:

CHAPTER 1

*N*ew Year's Eve had never been more than an afterthought in Dorset Hills. Christmas was the main event, and people put so much time and effort into making it special that they were happy enough to stand down till Valentine's Day. But this year, just before Christmas, a dognapping had changed everything. It was unthinkable that a crime like that could happen in Dorset Hills, a small city known as the best destination for dogs and dog-lovers across the country. For it to happen at Christmas was catastrophic, at least as far as City Council was concerned. Dogs were their brand, and dognappings were therefore bad for business. There was an immediate and unanimous vote to divert funds into damage control.

That was how New Year's Eve turned into a festival that attracted thousands of people and their dogs to Bellington Square outside City Hall on Saturday December 31st. Fireworks weren't an option, out of respect to the dogs, but an epic light show did a fine job of letting the community know that all was well again. There was something for everyone: live music, games, free food, and even a black-tie parade for dogs and their owners. It would be all over the news for days to come, and that was exactly the plan.

Marti Forrester was still in her office in City Hall when the revelry began. She normally did her best work after eight, when the lights automatically went out, but the noise and the pulsating, multicolor beams from the gathering outside gave her a headache. Her goal had been to ignore New Year's Eve completely, just as she had Christmas, but Council had made attendance mandatory for all staff. She could only avoid it so long.

Rubbing her temples, she read the same sentence over again. A lot hung on the presentation she was writing and she wanted to get every word right.

Her phone rang and she checked the time as she picked up. "Hey, Tonna."

"Marti, where are you?" Tonna asked. "I'm turning into a life-like ice sculpture."

"I'm only five minutes late," Marti said.

"Fifteen by the time you get here." Tonna was shouting, but only to be heard over the cacophony of music, voices and barking in the square. "Have mercy on my freezing butt."

"Where's Levi? Isn't your butt his business?"

Tonna laughed. "It sure is. But he got a last-minute gig, so I need you. Like you have a choice, anyway. Duty calls, my friend."

Putting the phone on speaker, Marti tapped out another bullet point. "I know. I'm just fine-tuning my pitch for Council."

"I'm sure it's perfect already."

"It needs to be better than perfect. I have to blow their socks off on Monday, so they'll greenlight the community health centers."

There was a pause at the other end, as if Tonna were choosing her words. "I know how important this is to you, Marti, but they've done a bait and switch on you before, no? You can't trust politicians."

"This time is different. It's my year. I can feel it."

"So you're saying that City Council has suddenly decided to make people a priority over dogs?"

Marti sighed. "Wrong galaxy, I guess. But the negative press over the dognapping could create an opportunity."

"That video, right? I can't stop watching it."

The video in question featured an animated Dorset Hills City Council singing 'The Twelve Days of Christmas' while a hooded thief came up behind them one by one and stole their dogs. The last dog to go was a Great Dane, and the thief had to hoist it over his shoulders while Council sang on. It was a satire of Council's blind adherence to Dog Town's brand, and so cleverly done that it went viral and made Dorset Hills even more famous. Only now that fame was tainted, and from all accounts the mayor was very unhappy.

"Council wants to fight back with good news," Marti said. "And what could be better than keeping kids and families healthy?"

"Oh Marti, you have such faith in Dog Town," Tonna said. "You need to be an outsider like me to see how ridiculous this place is."

"I see it, I just don't want to believe it. This is my hometown and I want to make a difference."

"I love that about you, but I worry, too. Especially after what happened with Oliver this year."

"Okay, I'm shutting down now," Marti said, pressing the computer's off switch.

Tonna's raucous cackle filled the office. "I figured that would get you moving. Oliver. Oliver. Ol-i-ver."

"You've entered the no-fly zone, my friend."

"So scared I'm shaking. Oh wait… that's hypothermia. Can we fight in person?"

Marti pulled her purse out of her desk drawer. "No fighting. This is going to be a banner year for both of us. I'll launch the health clinics, and you'll franchise your business."

"Right, shutting down now," Tonna said. "Touché."

Tonna was a true Dorset Hills success story. She'd arrived four years ago planning to make fun of Dog Town and ended up running an upscale dog club, called Beta Dogs.

"Seriously, it's now or never, Tons. Someone's going to steal your dream."

"If I'm dreaming don't wake me up. I just saw a dachshund in a pink strapless gown. Her owner was wearing the same thing, only over a parka."

Marti rolled her eyes as she put on her own parka. "Precious."

"Ditch that scorn, my friend. You're the face of the Dog Town regime."

"I'm a bureaucrat, not an elected official." Marti pulled up her hood and looped her scarf around it twice. "I do my best to steer clear of dog politics."

"On the bright side, this party is actually turning out to be fun."

"Yeah?" Marti dug through her purse for her mittens. "I'll be the judge of that."

There was a deep laugh from the doorway. Marti gave a scarf-muffled scream and dropped her purse. Coins, pens and lipstick jangled and rattled as they hit the floor.

A tall man was outlined against the light from the corridor. The door had been closed and spangled with a rainbow minutes earlier. How had she not heard it open?

"Ssssh, quiet. I'm not here," the man said.

"Who are you? What do you want?" Marti's voice quavered.

"Marti?" Tonna waited a beat, and then, "Marti!"

"Relax." The man took a step into her office. "It's just me."

Marti jumped backward, fell into her chair, and screamed for real this time.

Colored beams splashed over the man, but his face was shaded by a fedora. The weak backlight from the hallway behind made him look massive.

Scratch that. He *was* massive.

"Identify yourself right now," Tonna said. "This is not a game."

Tonna had the same commanding tone she used when breaking up a dog fight.

"Calm down, both of you," the man said.

His voice was familiar but Marti couldn't quite place it.

"That's it," Tonna said. "First, I'm going to scream my head off, and then I'm going to call the cops."

The man crossed the office and grabbed the phone with a gloved hand that seemed as large as a catcher's mitt. "You're quite the scrapper, young lady," he said.

Then he laughed, and the sound was rich and deep, like the voiceover on a luxury car commercial.

Marti and Tonna made the connection at the same time. "Mayor Bradshaw!"

"Quiet, ladies. Please. This visit is off the record." Stepping backward, he groped on the wall and then flipped the lights. He looked like a movie star, all angles and elegance. "I just wanted to catch up with Marti."

Tonna wasn't ready to roll over. "You scared us to death."

"I'm sorry, but you are—?" He waved the phone at Marti with a quizzical look.

"That's Tonna, sir," she said. "My best friend."

"Tonna," Mayor Bradshaw continued. "Lovely name. I apologize for interrupting, but I need to steal Marti for an hour or two."

"It's New Year's Eve! With all due respect, Mayor, Marti deserves a night off. She's been working herself into the ground on this community health business. She's Dog Town's Cinderella."

The mayor raised one salt-and-pepper eyebrow. "Well, maybe it's time for her fairy godfather to step in." He paused. "I'll deny I said that."

Tonna was laughing now. "Oh good, you're finally going to promote her."

A wave of heat rolled up from Marti's chest, and she shoved her hood back. "Tonna, please. I'm fine, Mayor Bradshaw."

He perched on the desk, his cashmere coat brushing Marti's knees. "Glad to hear it," he said, swinging one fine leather loafer. The socks Marti would need to blow off with her pitch were dotted with tiny gray schnauzers. "You've got a big year ahead."

A smile flashed across Marti's face. "I'm so excited. Working on the community health portfolio is such a privilege."

"It *is* a privilege to serve Dorset Hills, isn't it? I feel the same way."

"I was just polishing my presentation for Monday. I think you'll be—"

"That's next year," he said. "We have a few hours left in this one."

Marti gave him a quizzical look. "Then what did you want to talk about, sir?"

"It's a surprise." His green eyes twinkled. Marti sometimes thought his eyes had gotten him elected.

Tonna coughed conspicuously to remind him she was on the line. "Marti hates surprises, Mayor."

"She's right about that," Marti said. "We could set up a meeting with my director for Monday. He'd hate to be left out."

In the bureaucracy, there was a pecking order for reason: butt coverage. No matter what "surprise" the mayor had for Marti, it would be in the bare-butt arena. That was a dangerous place to be, even in a small community. *Especially* in a small community.

The mayor clapped his leather gloves. "This can't wait. Come with me, Marti."

"Sir, I can't—"

"—say no to me. Exactly. Your friend will have dinner on my tab at the Lone Dog Bistro while she waits."

After Tonna hung up, the mayor stood and gestured to the door. "Let's take a ride."

"That never ends well in movies, sir," Marti said, getting to her feet.

"This will be a glorious happily ever after," he said, crunching over the contents of her purse as he ushered her out the door. "Isn't that what you ladies like?"

"My happily ever after looks like three community health centers serving thirty thousand people a year."

"I admire your commitment." He guided her along the hall with one hand under her elbow. "Council has taken notice."

Dread began to percolate in Marti's stomach. Twelve years in government had shown her that being noticed led not to glory, but to more work—often work no one else would do. She stared around at the network of empty offices and dingy cubicles. City Hall at night felt like an empty hive filled with vague menace.

The security guards at the executive elevator nodded at her as she stepped ahead of the mayor. Inside, she looked down at her boots to avoid her reflection. Winter was never kind to her fine, blond hair, and her cheeks were pale. She hadn't been out much, except for the commute.

"A change will do you good, Marti," the mayor said. His face was bronzed and had very few lines for a man over 60.

"Noted, sir." She tried to smooth her hair with a mittened hand and made it significantly worse.

In the parking garage, two other security guards stood waiting by the mayor's black town car.

"Shall I drive, Mayor Bradshaw?" one man asked. "The traffic is crazy tonight."

The mayor dismissed the offer with a wave. "I've got it."

Marti slid into the passenger seat and struggled to buckle the seatbelt over her parka.

"Ready?" he asked.

Without waiting for an answer, he piloted the car out into the biggest street party Dorset Hills had ever seen.

CHAPTER 2

$\mathcal{T}$he crowds filling the streets parted for the mayor's car. People were dressed for the bitter cold, and even the dogs wore coats and little boots. The vote had been split on salting the roads, because it made dogs limp, but common sense prevailed. Winter was nothing to joke about in Dorset Hills, and traffic accidents weren't good for branding, either.

People bent to peer into the car but were thwarted by tinted windows. The mayor gave a wave just in case. It was like the campaigning never ended.

Marti looked back at City Hall. It was a graceful, old building that deserved better than being showered with silly lights. As a child she'd loved the clock tower, and she was even fonder of it now that it had begun to chime haphazardly. "Time marches to its own beat in Dorset Hills," newcomers joked. It was one of the quirky things that made this town charming, if only Council would leave well enough alone.

The mayor circled the square at a glacial pace so that they could take in the festivities. Fat flakes of snow had begun to fall, as if on cue. There had not been nearly enough snow at Christmas and people were hungry for it. Kids turned their faces to the sky and stuck out their tongues.

In the middle of Bellington Square sat the main attraction: a merry-go-round that featured not horses, but various breeds of dogs. As the spinning slowed, Marti made out a beagle, a boxer and a disproportionately large pomeranian. Those in line scrambled for their dog of choice; the dalmatian was the clear winner.

"Isn't that carousel something?" Mayor Bradshaw said. "We brought it in from Kansas City."

"Never seen anything like it," Marti said. A man hoisted his girlfriend onto a wolfhound and she teetered, giggling like a child.

"Which would you choose, Marti?"

It seemed like a casual question, but Marti knew everyone in Dorset Hills judged you by your breed preference. "The Bernese mountain dog," she said.

"Solid choice. Believe it or not, I'm a poodle man. You've heard about my Princess?"

Marti remembered Princess from the annual Dorset Hills wall calendar. "She's a parti, right? Black and white?"

"She's a party all right." He chuckled. "Smartest dog I've ever owned, but a handful. Took a lot of work with a good trainer to turn her into the model canine citizen she is now."

The car eased through the crowds in the children's activity area, where youngsters were bouncing and screaming on a huge inflatable dog bed. "Raising good fur-kids is challenging," Marti said.

"Especially after my wife passed," he said. "It was really her dog."

"I'm sure Princess is a huge comfort to you," Marti said.

Delores Bradshaw had been a key player in what qualified as high society in Dorset Hills until her death two years earlier. Soon after, the mayor sold his manufacturing business and threw his hat into the political ring. Now he seemed to be enjoying his second act, and it was probably just a matter of time before he married again. He wouldn't lack options.

"Do you have a dog, Marti?" he asked, braking for pedestrians who were so full of cheer that they didn't think twice before plunging off the curb.

"Not at the moment." She clasped mittened hands across her purse and sighed. "I work such long hours it wouldn't be fair."

"Understood." Cruising by food carts that dispensed hot dogs and steaming cocoa, he asked, "You hungry?"

Marti shook her head. Her stomach was knotted up to her throat. "I can't eat when I'm nervous."

"Nervous? There's nothing to be nervous about."

"I don't like surprises on principle, sir. I'm the type to be prepared."

"This surprise you're going to love. No preparation required."

Marti's hopes rose. "I've been living and breathing community health for two years. Guess I'm as prepared as I'll ever be."

"Exactly." He turned left at the corner and continued at a sedate pace along West Avenue. "Tell me more about life beyond work."

"Like Tonna said earlier, it's all work and no play these days."

"That must annoy your husband."

Marti froze for several seconds. "My husband?"

"Oliver, correct? I believe we met at the inauguration."

"Right, yes." She took a few slow breaths before responding. "Oliver is visiting his parents."

"What a shame he missed Christmas in Dorset Hills," the mayor said. "But he isn't from here originally, is he?"

"No, he's from Seattle, and he's there now. His mom has been ill."

The mayor gave Marti a quick look and her anxiety grew. It almost seemed like he'd been doing background checks on her, which made no sense. She was as squeaky clean as a workaholic bureaucrat could be.

"You'll be glad to see him back, I'm sure."

"Of course. The house seems…empty…these days." Her voice caught over the word and she closed her eyes for a second. She turned and practically pressed her nose to the window, hoping to deter the mayor from asking more questions.

Once they cleared the city center, the mayor picked up speed. "What do you think about this whole dognapping fiasco, Marti?"

"I think it'll die down soon. You'll announce some good news and people will forget."

His gloves squeaked as they tightened on the steering wheel. "They're not going to forget that video. It has three million hits."

"I'm not a politician, sir, but it seems like it's increasing awareness of Dorset Hills. Once people are curious, there's an opportunity…"

"To convert them," he said.

She laughed. "To show them how great our town is."

"I'm sure Pemsville's behind it," he said. "I've got people investigating."

Pemsville was one of many neighbouring cities that shared some of their beautiful countryside, but none of Dorset Hills' luck —or opportunism. People who couldn't afford Dog Town's real estate prices tended to buy property in Pemsville and bask in reflected glory.

"I guess we can't blame them for wanting a piece of the action," Marti said.

The mayor gave her the side-eye. "They can create their own action without undercutting ours."

"Fair enough, sir."

"What about this Mim Gardiner?" he asked. "The nurse whose dog got stolen. Do you know her?"

"She's been part of our consultations on community health. In fact, people have recommended Mim to lead one of the new centers. That could go a long way to changing the conversation."

The mayor snorted. "Mim Gardiner has a bad dog, Marti. She doesn't belong in a leadership position."

"George? He looked like a sweetheart."

"There were complaints on the Tattle Tail hotline about yapping, nipping and property damage."

"No dog is perfect, sir."

"Princess is perfect. We need more perfect dogs in Dorset Hills. Bad dogs lead to bad press."

Marti leaned forward as they neared Riordon Mill, hoping the car would slow down. She'd proposed the vacant site as the flagship community health center.

The car didn't slow down.

Speaking truth to power had never come easily to Marti, but she tried it now. "If you're asking for my opinion, sir…"

He gave her a genial smile. "Of course. That's why you're here."

"You may be barking up the wrong tree. Mim Gardiner was targeted by someone unbalanced who's been charged and dealt with. That should be the end of it."

"That's not the end of it. The city took a drubbing and we need to resuscitate our image."

"I know it's a cliché, but time cures all—"

"We don't have time. The dognapping came on the heels of that Thanksgiving Rescue Pageant fiasco."

It had been a rough couple of months for council and nerves were frayed. Marti wasn't sure what she was supposed to know, or if her information was even correct. She was really on the hot seat.

"Mayor, would you mind turning down the seat warmer, please?"

He didn't seem to hear the request. "That pageant almost blew up in our faces. You know that."

"Hardly anyone else does, though. Bridget Linsmore has kept that whole situation hush-hush, just as she was asked."

"I don't like the people she runs with. They call themselves the Rescue Mafia. Did you know that?"

Marti shifted her weight to one side to cool one butt cheek. "I heard they adopted that *after* the Canine Corrections Department coined the term."

"Doesn't matter." His expensive loafer pressed even harder on the gas. "Birdie promised me a feature about Dorset Hills on national TV. Where is it?"

"I'm sure Bridget is looking forward to seeing it too, sir. You know networks go quiet over Christmas. I'm sure it will air in the new year." She shifted her weight to the other cheek. "And then we'll be flooded with new residents who need health—"

"You know as well as I do that our success hangs on being the best place in the country for dogs. That means no bad dogs."

It had the ring of a slogan to it. "That's awfully hard to control, Mayor. It means no bad owners, really."

"Exactly. No bad owners, no bad dogs."

"Well, it sounds good in theory, but—"

"Glad you agree. Because you're an integral part of this plan."

"What plan?" Marti's voice went up an octave.

"Relax, it's all good news from here on in. Your hard work is about to be rewarded as Cinderella arrives at the ball."

Using just one finger on the steering wheel, he made a smooth turn onto Purley Crescent. The only building on the short street was the former legion, now known as the Dorset Hills Sporting Club. A dumpster sat out front beside a neat pile of lumber. The old coat of arms over the front door appeared to have been covered by a fresh coat of paint.

Bringing the sedan to a gentle stop, the mayor climbed out and walked around the car. He opened the passenger door and said, "Be careful where you step, Marti. It's mucky out here."

She stayed where she was. "I don't understand, sir."

Mayor Bradford leaned over and tugged gently on her arm. "Welcome to your new offices, director."

CHAPTER 3

*P*icking her way through the semi-frozen mud, Marti followed the mayor to the double front doors of the clubhouse. "Director of what?" she asked.

"Patience." He unlocked the door and pressed the key into her mitten. "All yours."

"I hate to sound ungrateful, sir, but this site's kind of out of the way for a community health clinic."

"True enough," he said, chuckling. "Just as well it's not a clinic then. And it's close enough to your home that you can walk to work on a nice day."

Inside, he found the light switch easily. Two rows of recessed lights flooded the long room. Marti had been to the club before for charity events and was shocked by the hasty renovation. The oak panelling had been either torn down or concealed by drywall, and the plank floor had been covered with industrial carpet. The thirty or so games tables had been replaced by a dozen standard-sized government cubicles and two glass-walled offices.

It was a brand new hive and apparently, she was the queen.

"I still don't understand," she said.

A wide smile lit the mayor's handsome face as he pointed to

the long sign leaning against the wall. Marti read it, and then tilted her head to read it again: Canine Corrections Department of Dorset Hills. The town crest, with its Labrador retriever surrounded by hills, sat on the upper right.

"You're expanding the CCD?" she said. It had been a small branch of six staff, including an investigations officer.

"We've come up with a new mandate for Dorset Hills: No Bad Dogs. To make that possible, we're allocating resources and designating a director. Namely, you."

"Uh, dogs are not my—"

He held up one hand. "You can't say no, Marti. We called an emergency meeting of the executive committee yesterday and you were given the nod. Simple as that."

"Cliff Whorley is the head of Canine Corrections."

"He's joining you, don't worry. But we needed a fresh take on the whole situation, and you've proven with your leadership on health care that you're the visionary we need."

"Health is what I know. What I'm passionate about. I've spent my whole career—"

"Sometimes life throws us a curveball that turns out to be the best thing that ever could have happened. This is quite an honor. Wait till you've had the full tour."

She followed him down the corridor, past the cubicles and a couple of boardrooms, to a large corner office. They'd retained the original paneling here, simply replacing the old girlie posters with prints of dogs. On the desk was a cardboard box. Marti gasped as she noticed a framed photo of Oliver. It had been in her bottom drawer at City Hall.

The mayor took the photo from the box and set it on the polished oak desk. "I had one of the guards collect your things and drop them off while we took the scenic drive," he said. "I wanted you to feel at home right away."

Marti's scarf felt like a noose that choked off her words. The mayor plucked a long, black garment off a coatrack before stepping out of the office and pushing open a heavy wood door. Switching on another light, he let Marti pass. "Come on, now. It's the pièce de résistance."

The legion's assembly hall, with tall windows on both sides, had been converted into something resembling a courtroom. On a dais, sat a sleek judicial bench bearing another coat of arms. Directly in front of the dais sat two columns of dark folding chairs.

"Arms up," the mayor commanded, and Marti did as she was told. He slid black robes over her parka.

She looked down and found her voice. "I'm a wizard?"

He laughed. "I hope you'll bring some magic to this role. Now, climb on up there." He nudged her toward the dais.

Marti took two steps up and perched on the leather chair behind the bench. A gavel sat to her right, and she ran her fingers along its polished handle. Finally, she asked, "Is this some kind of joke, sir?"

"Not at all. We'll be announcing your appointment as Executive Director of the CCD and Dog Court Judge on Monday. I suggest you read up on the new regulations tomorrow."

"I have no legal experience, sir. I'm a policymaker."

"It's sufficient," he said. "This isn't a real court of law. You know hearings for dog aggression and such aren't new to Dorset Hills. They just haven't been public."

"Dog problems aren't something we normally draw attention to in Dorset Hills," Marti said.

"Now we do. The No Bad Dogs regime is tough on dog crime. It's what we need to reclaim our position as the best destination for dog lovers in the country."

"We didn't lose that status over one dognapping," Marti said. "It will blow over soon, and community health is the perfect antidote for any bad press."

"You'll see my way is better soon. Hopefully with your first hearing on Monday at 10. It's a straightforward case of dog aggression. You'll expel the dog, we'll grab the headlines and get back on track."

"Expel?"

"No bad dogs, Marti. One strike and they're out of Dorset Hills."

"What? Where will these dogs go?"

"Rehomed. It's all in your dossier and I know you're a quick study."

"Yes, but the families—"

"There will be difficult moments, I'm sure, but the dogs who end up here will be trouble."

"Is there a—"

"In your dossier. I know you need to find your sea legs in politics, and I'll be coaching you every step of the way."

Marti's head spun and she was glad she was sitting down. Clearly, they'd stuck her in this role because she put duty first. She probably had a reputation as a yes-woman. But this didn't feel right at all.

Summoning her courage, she said, "I appreciate this honor, but I've devoted my professional life to health and I prefer to stay there."

"I'm afraid that's impossible."

"Impossible? Why?"

He swept his arm around theatrically. "This all cost money—money that was reallocated from the health division."

Marti gasped. "I've been downsized?"

"Of course not. You've been given the promotion you rightly deserve. But we did have to redirect funds from your former department into Canine Corrections. I've had to make some tough decisions for the city this week. But placing you in this role was an absolute joy."

"I can't—"

"—say no. Exactly. There's no going back now. But if you

17

distinguish yourself in this role, as I know you will, we'll put community health back on the table next year."

"But—"

"Nothing in life is free, Marti. You know that."

"I need to—"

"Get back downtown and meet Tonna. Yes, of course." He offered his hand to help her step down, and she needed the support. "I was impressed by your friend's dog club, by the way. Princess wants to visit."

He knew where she lived, and where Tonna worked. What else had he researched while she had her nose to the grindstone?

"There's just one more thing, Marti," he said, as he ushered her back into her new office. "Cliff Whorley isn't happy about the reorganization."

"No wonder. He's been head of the CCD for two years."

"Cliff's not judge material. He's a bulldozer in a bow tie."

"If he wants it—"

"Now, you on the other hand, have the common touch. You know how to win people over. I want your ear to the ground at all times. I'm counting on you to rehabilitate Dog Town's image."

She stared up at him. "And then you'll let me launch community health centers?"

"If you still want to." He switched off the lights as they went back out into the cold. "You can write your ticket after this. Six months is all I ask. A year tops."

Marti began to protest, but he hurried her along and practically shoved her into the car.

As he turned the key in the ignition she tried again. "Mayor, can we talk—"

"Now's not a good time, Marti," he said, pressing the pedal down. "I've got to plan my remarks for the midnight ball drop. I don't use a speechwriter, you know."

The sedan transformed into a rocket and roared back towards

the center of town. Bracing herself on the dashboard, Marti persisted. "Sir, I feel—"

"Nervous. I know. It's a major turning point in your career. But you'll learn on the fly, as most of us do."

"Okay, but—"

"You've got this." He squeezed her leg through her coat and Marti jumped.

"Sir." She was sure he didn't mean anything by that squeeze, but it was awkward just the same.

"Sorry," he said. "I'm just so excited about our new direction. Aren't you?"

"More like stunned."

"Take your time to get your bearings. And speaking of bearings… I know exactly what you need."

"I could really use a—"

"A bronze. Of course."

"A bronze?"

"A statue, Marti."

For the first time he sounded truly frustrated with her. The huge bronze dog statues sitting outside some institutions around town had become a popular attraction. In Bellington Square a fine pair of eight-foot German shepherds guarded city hall. Other breeds marked art galleries, museums, the fire station and the hospital. Some were funded by council and others by private donation. Public opinion among residents was split on the statues but tourism numbers had spiked and that was all the encouragement necessary.

"Let's not invest any more—" she began.

"Don't be silly. The CCD building absolutely needs at least one bronze outside. Name your breed, Marti and I'll make it happen."

"I couldn't begin to—"

His handsome face had gone stony and blank, at least in profile. "Fine, a Bernese Mountain Dog it is. We haven't used that one yet."

"My seat," Marti said. "It's hot. Very hot."

His face came to life again with a twitch of the lips. "Really."

Luckily, his phone rang before she had to explain.

For the rest of the ride, he listened to a detailed update from an advisor. Marti fell silent and stared out the window at the passing blur of Christmas lights. Council encouraged citizens to keep their lights on through February, at least. On the outskirts, a few renegades had strung up colored strings, rather than Council-sanctioned white. The closer they got to the city center, however, the whiter and more abundant the gleaming bulbs.

The mayor continued to talk on the phone even as he dropped her off at the bar to meet Tonna.

"Easy on the bubbly," he said, as she climbed out of the car. "You've got a lot of preparation to do tomorrow."

Marti leaned into the car. "Mayor Bradshaw—"

"You're welcome, Marti." He lifted his foot off the brakes. "See you Monday."

~

"You're sure you're okay?" Tonna said, as the cab pulled up to the curb outside Marti's house. The house was long and low, but it sat on a hill that got icy. "Maybe I should come in."

"I'll be fine," Marti said. "I'm going to heave, but I can manage that on my own."

"You only had two drinks," Tonna said. "I, on the other hand, had two too many. Damn the mayor and his open tab."

"Damn the mayor, indeed," Marti said.

Tonna elbowed her and gestured to the cab driver. "You mean, for being so damn generous."

Sighing, Marti pulled her wallet out of her bag and paid the driver. *Welcome to political life, where you don't have a thought to call your own.*

Tonna leaned in for a hug, and Marti squeezed her hard.

Neither of them were the huggy type, but tonight she needed it. "This sucks so bad," Marti whispered. "He wouldn't let me finish a sentence."

"It'll be all right, my friend. I got your back."

Marti nodded. That was the only thing she felt sure about as she got out of the cab. "Happy new year, Tonna."

"Shaping up to be a wild one," she said, as the door closed.

Marti was halfway up the driveway before she realized something wasn't quite right. Normally the steep slope would be treacherous after an inch of snow. It looked like it had been shovelled earlier. In fact, there was a crunch of salt underfoot.

Stopping dead, she looked up. The lights were on throughout the house. That could only mean one thing: Oliver.

She hurried up the stairs, fumbled to unlock the door and flung it open. "Oliver?"

Silence.

Walking from room to room, she saw no proof that her husband had actually surfaced after seven weeks. Finally, she followed her nose to her home office. There, on her desk, sat a vase holding a large bouquet of fragrant pink freesia.

So, he'd come home with her favorite flowers on New Year's Eve to find the house empty. And now he was gone again without so much as a note or a text.

This year was full of surprises already. And she still hated surprises.

CHAPTER 4

*M*arti's nose was running from the combination of the smell of fresh paint and the wintery breeze leaking in through the old windows of the courtroom. She sniffed, knowing she'd never be able to find the tissue in her pocket under her new robes. Curling her icy fingers into fists, she tried to focus on the din of voices around her.

"Judge?"

The voice came from the front row of the folding chairs on the left side of the room. There were two sections, each five chairs wide and eight rows deep. Marti hoped there would never be a full house. It already felt crowded with 14 people.

"Judge? Marti?"

The familiar voice snapped Marti out of her trance. "Yes, Vince," she said, glancing at the speaker. "I mean, Mr. Bertucci."

She'd known Vincent since high school, when they'd been on student council together. Back then, his dark eyes, thick hair and tall frame had been enough to make her look forward to those meetings. Now, he looked older than his 36 years. Although his hair was still dark, he was faded and pinched. She wondered if he was thinking the same about her. After two nights with little sleep, she felt faded and pinched. Worse, she felt ridiculous. The robes and the dais were a bit much, let alone the gavel at her right hand. As if she would ever use that.

"Judge, I asked if the testimony of her witnesses counted," Vince said. "They're obviously all friends."

There was a shuffle of indignation on the right side of the room, and one chair scraped against the newly stained oak floors. "Excuse me. While I certainly know all my clients, we are not friends. Even my friends are afraid to come to my shop because of you."

Lotus Fiore glared over at Vince and then up at Marti. Her long, bushy hair was tied back, but a few curly tendrils floated on the breeze, making her look like a bohemian Medusa. She pushed up the sleeves of her T-shirt under a tasselled poncho. Even from 10 feet away, Marti could identify at least six different dog tattoos. The needle-nosed Corgi above Lotus' wrist seemed quite good.

Marti knew Vince was right about the "witnesses." Whenever she passed Lotus' shop, Crackers (the lettering on "Crack" was twice the size of the rest of the word), she saw the same gaggle of people in the little courtyard with their assorted crossbreeds. The fact that they all owned rescue dogs was probably a point of pride. In a town where the breed you owned defined who you were, choosing a rescue declared you were an outsider.

Or in this case, an aspiring outsider. "Lotus" had been raised as Laura Fordham in a nice house a few blocks from where Marti grew up. Laura dropped out of school, disappeared for 15 years, and made her way back to Dorset Hills when the town's reputation for being a dog mecca started to grow. She took over the shoe repair store at the stodgy end of Main Street and opened a vegan dog biscuit bakery.

Vince's shop, Bertucci's Fine Italian Meats, sat directly opposite Crackers. He'd worked with his dad in the shop since he was a kid, and took over when Vincent Sr. died. Bertucci's was what people called "old school," meaning it predated Dorset Hills' transformation from a quaint but average small city into "Dog Town." As new residents moved in with their dogs, businesses sprang up to support them. Bertucci's struggled to compete, although it was still known as the purveyor of the best prosciutto around.

The defendant today wasn't Vince, but Guido, the brindle Italian mastiff who sat between his feet. With his closely cropped ears and beefy jowls, Guido was a homely dog, at least in Marti's eyes. He'd always seemed like a sweetheart, though, and welcomed everyone into the shop like a doorman.

Lotus had filed a complaint against Guido, saying that he'd charged across the street and bitten one of her customers. The customer in question, another long-time resident, had declined to press charges. Lotus persisted with her case, saying she was losing business because people were terrified to visit Crackers in case Guido struck again.

"I have news for you," Vince said to Lotus now. "If business is slow it's because dogs don't like lentils and hay. They're carnivores."

"They're omnivores," Lotus shot back. "They can successfully live as vegetarians, and my dog does."

"Survive and thrive are two different things," Vince said.

"I suppose yours thrives on a steady diet of fat and sulphites?"

"People." Marti raised her voice to be heard. "Listen up. You are in a courtroom."

"Sorry, Judge," Vince said.

"Just keep things civil, and stick to the point, please. Mr. Bertucci, there are four witnesses here saying Guido mouthed the lady in question."

"Bit her," Lotus corrected.

"If she refused to press charges, I suspect you're overstating the aggression," Marti said. Scanning the group, she pointed to a woman in jeans and a parka. Except for her extremely long hand-knitted scarf, she was pretty low on the Bohemian scale. "Ma'am, please step forward."

The woman approached the dais, and Marti looked down, trying to hold her gaze so that she wouldn't be influenced. "Can you tell me what you saw on the afternoon of December 14th, outside Crackers?"

Lotus raised her hand but Marti ignored it and continued. "Guido came across the street…" she prompted. "And the woman in question was… What? Leaving Crackers?"

The witness twisted her scarf and tried to turn toward Lotus. Marti said, "Just look at me, please. Had the woman in question been in Crackers?"

"No, judge."

"Did it appear that she intended to go into Crackers?"

"I… I don't think so. I think she was just walking by."

Lotus called out, "You don't know that. She was carrying a dog."

"As are many Dorset Hill residents, Ms. Feore," Marti said. "So this woman was just walking by carrying her dog, and the accused did what?"

"Guido—I mean, the accused—sort of stood on his hind legs to sniff the dog."

"And then…?"

"The little dog snapped at him."

"So, then the accused…?

"Snapped back, I guess."

"And bit his owner by accident?"

"Her bag, actually. Guido snagged her bag and gave it the death shake. Her stuff went flying everywhere. She was screaming, and dropped her dog and it went after Guido."

"And Guido...? I mean, the accused?" Marti asked.

"He ran back across the street. With her wallet."

"Which I returned immediately," Vince called.

Marti raised her hand to Vince. "And everyone helped pick up the woman's things?"

The witness nodded. "Lotus came out with a biscuit for her dog."

Vince called out, "And what did the dog do?"

"Mr. Bertucci, I'm doing the questioning here." Marti turned to the witness. "What did the dog do?"

"He lifted his leg on it and hit Lotus' sleeve."

Marti closed her eyes for a second and willed herself not to laugh.

Vince did laugh, but it sounded hollow. "I rest my case," he said.

Opening her eyes, Marti said, "You're the defendant, Vince. At any rate, what I'm hearing, Ms. Feore, is that this woman was just passing your store with no apparent interest in entering, and her dog initiated the aggression with the accused."

Lotus stepped forward unbidden. "Well, first, you don't know that she wasn't planning on shopping at Crackers." She turned and jabbed a finger toward Guido. "And second, that monster should never have been near my store."

"He's *not* a monster." The tremulous voice belonged to Lina, Vince's nine-year-old daughter. "Daddy?

Sensing the tension in the air, Guido lifted his head, sniffed, and raised his lip. Marti saw the flash of fang and hoped she was the only one who did.

"Aha! Did you see that, Judge?" Lotus' voice rang out over the victorious murmur of her posse. "He's vicious."

"He knows you're attacking his family," Vince said. "Mastiffs are intuitive and highly loyal. He can tell you're trying to put me out of business and starve my kids."

"Oh, please," Lotus said. "All I want is peace and harmony. So get yourself a civilized dog." Egged on by her posse, she added, "And feed it a vegan diet."

Vince stood up, and Guido followed suit. "Look here, Boho. If I waved bacon in front of your stupid mutt, he'd do every trick he knows to get a taste. If he knows any tricks."

"My dog doesn't do tricks," Lotus said. "He's not a circus clown."

"If you people had your way, dogs would have the vote in Dorset Hills."

Lotus pushed her sleeves up over the elbows in a dramatic gesture. "If you're saying I think dogs deserve to be treated like kings, I'm guilty as charged."

"Dogs are dogs," Vince said. "What happened to make you feel like they're more important than people?"

The outrage was like a sudden brushfire. People jumped to their feet, and in the confusion, Guido's leash slipped out of Vince's hand. The dog ran over and grabbed a tassel hanging from the bottom of Lotus' poncho. He pulled back until Lotus teetered and then tipped into the folding chair beside her, which collapsed. Vince snapped his fingers and Guido was back by his feet in a flash, but the tassel was dangling from his jaws.

The uproar from the plaintiff's side was deafening. Marti considered yelling for quiet, but didn't want to get Guido any more excited. Instead, she reaching for the gavel and brought it down once. The first whack barely made a sound.

The second was louder, and still everyone ignored it.

The third felt like it would snap her wrist, but it worked. The room became silent and everyone looked up at her expectantly.

"Sit down," she said. "And let's start taking this seriously."

MARTI'S OFFICE was an island of sterile calm after the courtroom, at least until the mayor walked in a few minutes later.

The CCD staff stopped unpacking their boxes to stare after him.

"You did the right thing, Marti," he said, moving a box off her guest chair so he could sit.

"Really? Vince is losing his dog. That doesn't feel right at all." Marti's voice cracked and she looked down at her hands; they were reddened from the chill of the courtroom. The mayor rose and closed her door. "Now, now. Don't get all emotional on me, Marti. One reason I gave you this role is that you never lose your cool. Your objectivity is rare, even in the civil service."

Marti had been called a cold fish before, but this was the first time it was a compliment. She took a deep breath and then stood to remove her robes.

"Don't. We're expecting a guest. I've set up an interview with the *Dorset Hills Expositor*. And here she is now."

Leslie Longland wasn't the scruffy young reporter Marti expected. She was a willowy blonde in her forties whose blue eyes never left the mayor, even as she pelted Marti with questions.

"What makes you right for this job, Ms. Forrester?" she asked.

Marti hoped Mayor Bradshaw would answer, but he just nodded encouragingly. "Well, I've lived in Dorset Hills all my life, except for college," she told the reporter. "So, I know this community in and out. On top of that, I have twelve years' experience in government, most recently in community health."

"Right. What happened to the community health center proposal?" Leslie asked.

"Good question," Marti said, glancing at the mayor. He raised a warning eyebrow and she continued, "Sometimes tough decisions need to be made. We've decided to defer the centers until we can get everything right. Just for a few months."

The mayor stepped in then. "I speak for the entire Council in saying we could not be more pleased with our choice of director of Canine Corrections. Marti Forrester is a true leader and team player, and she keeps a level head no matter what."

After that, he took all the questions, and kept talking to Leslie long after Marti had excused herself to throw up in the restroom. She'd always had a sensitive stomach, but since her promotion it had turned into Old Faithful.

~

THICK SLEET WAS FALLING by the time Marti locked up the Courthouse and headed for the parking lot. It felt strange to be working anywhere other than City Hall after all these years. There hadn't been room there for the expanded CCD, so Council had offered a generous incentive to move the men's sports club. This was one of the few old buildings in Dorset Hills to have the desired gravitas for the Canine Corrections proceedings.

She'd learned a lot about so-called dog crime as she worked through the official dossier. It had been a surprise to discover that hearings had increased from a handful to more than a hundred over the past few years. Initially, the cases were mostly about aggression, but now it seemed like anything was fair game. Such was the new age of Dog Town.

Although there was more to the CCD than she'd expected, Marti sensed cracking down on dog crime wasn't the answer. After all, more families and dogs moved into the city every year, and density created a problem in and of itself. Sure, dogs could run free on the trails in the hills, but most people didn't give them that opportunity. Frustrated dogs caused problems, as Marti was only beginning to understand from the files on her desk.

She'd started the day feeling that the weight of Dog Town's reputation rested on her shoulders, and ended it worried about the canine citizens. People could be ruled with guidelines and bylaws and old-fashioned shaming. Dogs, on the other hand, were just dogs. Sometimes, their owners lost control for one reason or another. This manifested in a variety of happenings that rarely made the news. In fact, Marti suspected there'd been a tacit agreement with the media to downplay dog crime in the interest of expanding the community. Something had changed recently, and she suspected it had a lot to do with the anonymous Tattle Tail hotline. Now the old guard—not all of them dog crazy—could rat out their neighbors with impunity. If they didn't see action, they threatened to take their complaints public. The CCD had never been busier.

In time, she hoped to come up with a policy solution that would put dog court out of business. It wasn't what she'd wanted, but it was a worthy cause, and easier to tackle from the inside, she figured.

Tonight, she felt overwhelmed as she splashed across the parking lot in tall rubber boots.

A dark shape moved out of the shadows beside Marti's Jeep. "Who's there?" she demanded, stopping.

"It's just me. Vince," the man said. "Sorry to startle you."

Marti pushed back her hood to get a better look at him. She would ask Council to add more lighting back here. "What is it, Vince?"

"What is it? You just took my dog away from my family, Marti."

"I had no choice. Guido's actions were aggressive. In Dog Court, no less."

"He pulled a pom-pom off Boho's poncho. That's aggressive?"

Marti sighed. "It wasn't in play, Vince, and you know it."

"He didn't bite anyone, and *you* know it."

"The new regulations are clear. Any type of aggression is actionable."

"Then why not issue a muzzle order?"

Muzzles were banned now, too; they sent the wrong message. "You wouldn't want Guido in a muzzle all the time, Vince."

"It would be better than losing him."

The anguish in his voice sent Marti reeling backwards a couple of steps. "I'm so sorry, Vince." Remembering the mayor's order to remain detached, she added, "But you know the new mandate: there's zero tolerance for aggression."

"Right," he said, dully. "No bad dogs."

"Guido will be okay," she said, fighting to keep her voice steady.

The scene as Guido was led away by CCD officers had been heart-wrenching. Marti had recessed court and sent the Crackers posse away so that the Bertucci family could have a last moment with their dog. Vince's wife and daughters were all sobbing, and Marti had fled to avoid doing the same.

"Where are they taking him?"

"I really can't say, Vince. The CCD is still developing its plans. But I can tell you he will be treated well."

"They're taking him to Pemsville, aren't they?"

"It will be further away than that, Vince. But the regulations are clear that no dog will be harmed."

"Because that would be more bad press for Dog Town."

She ignored this. "In time, Guido will adjust."

"What about us? How will we adjust? My kids are distraught. And my wife… she thinks this is my fault. That I should have watched him better."

Marti didn't know what to say, so she unlocked her car and took a step towards it. "Vince, I am sorry. I had no choice."

"My family is falling apart and that's all you can say?"

Opening the door, she turned to him. "Your family is stronger than one dog."

He rubbed sleet off his face and shook his head. "I'm not so sure. My business has taken a hit with all this new age dog stupidity. A business my dad put thirty years into is losing out to vegan dog biscuits."

"There's been a lot of change, I know," Marti said, sliding into the driver's seat. "You do have the right to appeal, remember."

"And you'll drag it out till my shop is shuttered and my house is empty." He glanced back at the courthouse. "You even took my club."

"Appeal, Vince. You never know what can happen." As she closed the car door, she added, "Dogs have long memories."

She thought it would help, but it looked like Vince was wiping more than sleet away from his eyes as he straightened his shoulders and walked away.

CHAPTER 5

*M*arti sat inside her parked car staring at her house for five minutes before finding the courage to go inside. The driveway was salted again, and the lights were on. She could see Oliver's SUV parked across the road. Apparently, several tough conversations weren't enough for one day.

Getting through the door proved to be the easy part. After that, she felt three points of contact as she fell—her shoulder, the back of her head and one hip. The pain didn't have time to register before a face loomed over hers and started licking.

Not Oliver.

Hank.

If the crushing pressure on her ribcage was any indication, Hank was closing in on his projected adult weight of 100 pounds. That was about the only assessment she could make as he slobbered over every inch of her face.

"Guess he remembers you." It was Oliver's voice, but she couldn't see him through the black, brown and white screen of frenzied Bernadoodle.

"Dogs really do have long memories," she said, finally managing to push Hank off.

Oliver offered his hand to help her to her feet. "You okay?"

She assumed he meant physically, from the fall, and not emotionally from his abrupt departure in November after eight years of marriage. Either way, the answer was the same. "I'm not sure."

She felt the back of her head and checked her hand for blood. Nothing. Everything else seemed fully functional, although there would be bruises. Accepting Oliver's hand, she clambered to her feet. Hank continued to make dancing advances on her, licking her hand, mouthing her pant leg, grabbing her sleeve. Just generally being annoying, which was what Hank did best. He might be larger and even more gorgeous than when she saw him last, but he apparently hadn't matured much.

"What are you doing here?" Marti's eyes dropped to the back-pack—the same one Oliver had toured Europe with after college —open on the living room floor. Did he think he could just waltz back in here and pick up where they'd left off? Sure, he'd continued to pay his share of the bills while he was gone, including adding to the emergency fund, which she'd needed when the pipes froze in December, but seriously, did he think that was enough? Why hadn't she changed the locks? Sent his money back? Now she'd have to deal with whatever had made him leave in the first place. She wasn't entirely sure what that was and preferred to go on without ever being edified. He could have stayed gone for all she cared. Except that eventually, people would realize he wasn't just visiting his parents. They'd stop thinking she was a supportive wife and start thinking she'd been dumped. Dorset Hills was full of gossips, and it wasn't just dogs they talked about. As a member of the Old School, and a newly christened judge in the New School, she was fair game for all.

"Hello to you, too," Oliver said, with a twisted smile.

She knew that smile. It meant he was already dismissing how she felt. Pushing Hank out of the way, she went over to the hall mirror. Obviously the goose egg growing on the back of her head didn't show, but it gave her something to do while she gathered her wits.

Behind her, Oliver's smile faded. It seemed like there was a little more grey in his hair, which had been silvering since his mid-twenties. His eyes were bright and blue, and he was as handsome as ever, but it didn't matter now.

Turning to him, she started over. "Hello, Oliver. What *are* you doing here? I've asked you about your plans before and never gotten an answer. Now, you just...show up."

"I showed up on New Year's Eve. Only to find you were out and not taking calls."

"It was business. I was out with the mayor."

"Ah, Bill. He's always had a thing for you."

"That's ridiculous. He's nearly old enough to be my father."

Again with the twisted smile. "Like that ever stopped a guy."

"Oliver, what's going on? Are you really... back?" It took some effort to spit out the word. She hadn't wanted him to go and hadn't wanted him to stay. Confusion was churning around in her stomach in much the same way as Hank was churning through Oliver's backpack.

She gestured to the dog, but Oliver continued to stare at her. "Temporarily," he said. "I'm going to a writing camp."

He had always wanted to write, but the money he made in IT was too good to give up—particularly when his employer had agreed to let him work from home or apparently wherever he liked. She'd tried to encourage him to pursue his dream, but it took leaving her to make it happen. "Camp? In January?"

"A workshop then. A retreat."

A seed of suspicion took root and grew faster than Hank had in his unbelievable early growth spurt. "Where?"

"Not far. And it's only two weeks."

Oh no. No, no, no. "Oliver, you can't."

"Of course I can. I have to—I've paid in full."

"What about Hank?"

Turning, Oliver pried open Hank's jaws and pulled out a sopping, half-chewed energy bar. "Hank's staying with you."

"That's impossible."

Oliver tossed the remains on the bar on a high shelf and laughed. "Impossible? He's your dog."

"Clearly he's not my dog. You took him and left."

"You chose him. Brought him halfway across the country, no less."

This part was true. When Oliver had started dropping hints about having kids, she'd proposed a dog instead. He took the bait, and they'd waited more than a year for their number to come up on a reputable breeder's list. By then, however, their marriage had developed a wobble.

Marti had hoped Hank would bring them closer, but the pup had the opposite effect. Oliver had worked hard on training all day and complained that Marti came home and undid everything by spoiling Hank. That was probably true, too. As Oliver withdrew, she'd turned to Hank for affection. They'd taken a dysfunctional turn, and by the time Hank was a belligerent teen, it was clear that they had a big problem on their hands. Hank jumped on people, answered to his name only if he was in the mood, and pulled so hard on the leash that neither wanted to walk him. On top of all that, he'd had major surgery twice to remove a ball and an unidentifiable foreign body from his gastrointestinal tract, taking a good chunk out of their savings.

The wobbly marriage quietly collapsed one day. Marti came home to find Oliver packed and ready to visit his parents. He claimed his dad was a dog whisperer who could turn Hank around. Marti had locked her feelings down and bitten her tongue.

"You said you were going to leave Hank with your parents," she said now.

"Only till he settled down. He has settled down."

Hank was taste-testing the coffee table leg he'd broken months earlier. If he had improved, there was a long way to go.

"It broke my heart, Oliver."

"You don't even like Hank."

"I always loved Hank! I just couldn't handle that much dog. I was wrecking him, just like you said. But I didn't want you to take him away, even to fix him."

"That's not why I left, anyway," Oliver said, starting to stuff his belongings into his backpack. "And you know it."

They'd never fought much, which Marti used to consider a good thing. Now she realized how much had been going on in that silence. It took some nerve to say now, "I don't actually know why."

His glance was a slash from a blue scythe. "Because you were cheating on me."

She gasped. "I *never*!"

"You were obsessed with your job," he added quickly. "After we got Hank you just worked longer and longer hours. I was like the mom at home with a new baby and you never helped."

"Health was a huge project, Oliver. My dream come true. You know that."

He yanked on the backpack's drawstring until it snapped. Swearing quietly, he knelt and fiddled with it, tying a knot. Hank came over and nuzzled his cheek. "Thanks, buddy," he said, leaning his head into the dog's flank briefly.

Marti watched, surprised by how their bond had deepened.

Standing, Oliver reached for his coat, which was on the back of the chair where he always tossed it. That had bothered Marti when they were together. Tonight she put her hand on it to keep him from going.

He misread the gesture. "You only have to keep the dog for two weeks. Surely you can handle that?"

She wanted to say yes, she'd do that for him. But what came out was, "I have a new job. Hank might be a liability."

Oliver sighed. "What now?"

When she told him, he laughed out loud. "Are you kidding me? A judge in dog court?"

"More like an arbitrator, I guess."

"What exactly are you judging? Poop infractions?"

"Canine aggression, and much more. It's an important job."

"Oh please, it's a farce. What happened to health care reform? *That* was an important job."

"Delayed," she said, fighting to stay neutral. "This is a promotion, and I'm lucky to get it."

"You don't believe that."

She closed her eyes for a second. "I believe in making the best of a bad situation. The mayor said if I did this, he'd make health a priority in a year."

Oliver shook his head. "And you believed that?"

"I had no choice."

"There's always a choice. Marti, you're many great things, but you're uniquely ill-equipped to judge problem dogs. I bet you can't even issue a muzzle order. You're too soft."

"There won't be any muzzles in Dog Town," Marti said. "Zero tolerance for dog misbehaviour."

He leaned on the chair and evaluated her. "Then what happens to bad dogs?"

She looked down at her hand, still clutching his jacket. "They're rehomed. Bad dogs are bad for Dog Town."

Oliver fell silent and she looked up to see a stunned look on his face. He'd never loved Dorset Hills, and only agreed to move there because Marti wanted to be closer to her dad. It was meant to be short-term, but as time passed, Marti, at least, became entrenched.

Finally, he jerked the coat out from under her hand. "If you can ban dogs, I guess you're not as soft as I thought."

Marti held onto the sleeve, infuriated. So she was either too soft, or not soft enough. She couldn't win. "Look, it may seem silly to you, but this is my reality right now."

"Did you consider saying no? For once in your career?"

"That's not fair."

He pulled the sleeve out of her hand and shrugged into his coat. Taking something out of his pocket, he reached for her hand and folded her fingers around it. Hank's leash.

"That's your reality, too," Oliver said. "I have full confidence that you can get through two weeks without banishing your own dog."

"Wow. You're an ass. I wished I'd realized that sooner."

"Maybe you should have paid more attention," he said, striding for the door.

Hank followed him and shoved himself between the Oliver and the door. "Not this time, buddy." Oliver leaned down and planted a kiss between Hank's ears. "Be good. Or give it your best shot."

"Oliver, wait."

Opening the door, Oliver blocked it with one knee. "By the way, don't plan on watching TV tonight. Hank got to the remote before I did."

With one deft move, he shoved Hank backwards, slipped out of the house, and closed the door.

Hank sat down, threw his head back and gave a heart-rending howl. Grabbing his collar, Marti opened the door. Oliver had crossed the street to his car.

"Oliver, please," she called. He didn't turn before climbing into the car and there was a squeal as the wheels spun on the ice.

Hank lunged and twisted to break her grip on his collar and then ran out the door. As Oliver drove up the street, Hank galloped after him. The high-pitched howls ripping out of his throat were like nothing Marti had ever heard before.

She skidded down the stairs and ran after him.

CHAPTER 6

"*T*hat is just heartbreaking," Tonna said, pulling a bottle from the wine rack and twisting off the cap. "How long till you caught him?"

"Three blocks," Marti said, easing onto a high stool at the end of the smooth marble counter. Tonna's newly remodelled kitchen was a nice blend of classic old wood and modern stainless appliances. "He sat down in the middle of an intersection and wailed. I wanted to do the same."

Tonna, tall, lithe and effortlessly graceful, reached for the glasses she kept on the top shelf of the cupboard. "I'm surprised Oliver held out this long. He's crazy about you, Marti."

"Pardon me? Did you hear anything I said?"

Setting the glasses on the counter, Tonna started to pour. "Yep. I heard that poor man was butt-hurt over your neglect and left town to make you realize what you had."

"Interesting interpretation. That man stole my dog and ran home to his daddy. And that left me a sitting duck for City Council. There's no way they'd have targeted me if they'd known about Hank."

Shaking her head, Tonna slid a glass across the counter to

Marti. "Well, Oliver wants to make it right. That's why he showed up on New Year's Eve with your favorite flowers. You were out partying and his pride took another hit."

"Another interesting spin. The flowers were meant to butter me up so I'd keep Hank while he writes his opus."

Tonna was pouring her own wine when a savage screech from the next room made her arm spasm. A pool of deep red raced along the counter and began to drip onto the floor.

Three strides carried Tonna into the family room. She returned carrying Diva, a cairn terrier. Hank ambled behind them, a dopey expression on his striking face. Marti couldn't believe how close his markings came to those of the Bernese. His coat was fluffy and non-shedding, a gift from his poodle mom. His personality appeared to be a careful blend of the negative traits of each parent—the stubbornness of the Bernese and the frantic energy of the poodle. Oliver said she'd been taken for a ride with this hybrid, but Marti suspected they'd have made a mess of any dog.

Diva wasn't perfect either. Far from it. She had the terrier determination with a dash of drama queen. She'd killed a few squirrels when they took her out in the hills, and couldn't be trusted at the exclusive dog club and day care Tonna owned lest she mistake a puppy for a rodent. Members paid an annual membership fee to be able to mix and mingle with good dogs and good people. While the situation was ideal for taking one's dog to work, Tonna ended up saying Diva had chronic hip pain that kept her at home. In Dog Town, it was easier to fake a canine ailment than admit you had a behavioural problem on your hands.

After Marti mopped up the wine, Tonna set Diva on the counter, where she settled so quickly it was obvious she'd spent time there before. Hank ran his nose along the edge of the counter and Diva sprang to life with a lunge and snap. Most dogs probably would have taken a hint, but not Hank. He simply circled around and came back. Marti and Tonna sipped their wine in silence as this played out. Only after the fourth snap did Hank give up and head over to examine Diva's food bowl. It was long since emptied, but Diva yapped warningly anyway.

"What am I going to do, Tonna? Can you help?"

Tucking butterscotch-colored hair behind her ear, Tonna took a deep gulp of her wine. "Marti, you know I'd do anything for you. Except Hank."

"But I can't keep him. Imagine the headline: 'Dog Court Judge has Bad Dog.'"

"I'm already skating on thin ice," Tonna said. "Together, these two would destroy me. No one would have any confidence that I could keep their dogs from killing each other."

Marti set her glass down and pressed both hands into her forehead. "I know. Sorry I asked. I just didn't know what else to do."

"Say no to Oliver, maybe?"

"He didn't give me a choice," Marti said.

"You explained about your job?"

"I did, and he laughed." She opened a drawer and started rearranging the cutlery. "I don't really blame him. It sounds ridiculous."

"It is ridiculous. But it's one of the highest profile jobs in Dorset Hills. Council will give you whatever you want after this."

That's what Marti had been telling herself since her dubious promotion. But the truth was that she'd already had what she wanted in health reform.

"I hate Dog Court," Marti said. "Today I had to send away a dog. The family is busted up."

"Guido Bertucci, I know. Everyone was talking about it at the club."

"Great. Just great." Marti started to pat Diva, who lifted her lip in a silent snarl. "No offense, Tonna, but your dog's a bitch."

Tonna laughed. "She is that. You should see her with Levi.

Hates his guts." Tonna hadn't talked much about Levi, which meant he probably had potential.

"So, what am I going to do about Hank?" Marti asked.

Tipping the last of her wine into her mouth, Tonna swallowed. "I have an idea."

$\approx$

SIX PHONE CALLS LATER, Tonna refilled their wine glasses. "I can't believe all of the good pet resorts in Pemsville said no. Business has to be slow in January. The second they heard Hank's not neutered they shut me down."

Marti had been impressed that Tonna had made such a convincing argument for late neutering when she wasn't a proponent herself. Even with evidence amassing that it was better for large breeds, delaying the snip hadn't caught on in Dorset Hills. Unneutered dogs got a bad rap for causing tension. As far as Marti could tell, testosterone wasn't to blame for Hank's problems.

"Maybe I should take him in and have him snipped while Oliver's away," she said. "He's a year now."

"Then you'd have to keep him very quiet for two weeks. This dog needs regular workouts."

Hank had collapsed on his side with one of Diva's chew toys, taking up most of the kitchen floor space. He cast surreptitious glances at Diva, and she rewarded him with occasional growls.

"I'll find a reputable walker to take him into the hills every day and wear him out."

"That's all you can do," Tonna said.

"And if trouble finds Hank, as it so often does, I'll develop an issues management plan, just like at work. Complete with key messages."

Tonna raised her glass in a toast. "That's thinking like a leader.

You can put the blame squarely on Oliver's parents for spoiling him while he was gone."

"Fall guys. I like it," Marti said. "The mayor did tell me to start thinking like a politician. Just the same, I'd prefer to keep Hank under cover. People will ask too many questions."

Marti topped up their glasses. She screwed the lid back onto the wine bottle, knowing full well they'd finish the last few inches soon. They made it a policy to finish whatever they started, and since they lived only a few blocks apart, they could always walk home.

Reaching for Hank's leash, Marti leaned over to hook him up. "Maybe I'll ask the vet for tranquillizers."

"You can't drug your dog, Marti."

"Got a better idea?"

"Maybe."

Tonna picked up the phone again and pressed hands-free. "Hi, Cori. I'm calling you with another referral."

"Great, I appreciate the business." The woman's voice was clipped and professional. "What've you got?"

"So one of my clients got dumped with an unruly bruiser for a week. A Bernese mutt." Tonna smirked at Marti. "She wants to get him some in-board training while he's in her care."

"I cut my in-board program, Tonna. I'd get the dog trained up perfectly but I couldn't train the owners to maintain it. So the dogs would slide back."

"Just this one time?" Tonna pleaded. "It would mean so much to my friend."

"Even if I wanted to, I couldn't. With this No Bad Dogs regime, everyone's trying to clean up their training issues. I'm booked solid as it is."

"People are jittery, I guess."

"Especially after Vince Bertucci today. Unbelievable. If I get five minutes with that judge, I'm gonna—"

"I hear you," Tonna said. "Council gave her a tough role, though."

"Well, she could have said no. That would have been the right thing to do."

Marti winced, and Tonna patted her shoulder.

"Then someone else would have said yes," Tonna told Cori. "Someone worse than Marti Forrester. She's a reasonable person, from what I can tell."

"Sending that cane corso to a farm in Brenton is reasonable?"

"A farm sounds nice."

"More like a concentration camp. Besides, corsi are intensely loyal dogs and difficult to rehome. He'll likely become seriously depressed."

Marti unscrewed the cap from the wine bottle and raised it to her lips.

"Okay," Tonna said. "I'll take that as a no. But thanks."

"I do have a message for your friend, though," Cori said. Marti lowered the bottle to listen. "Tell her if she wants to work with this Bernese mutt one on one, I'll help her. There are no shortcuts in training and that kind of thinking is probably what got her into trouble in the first place."

Tonna hung up and held out her hand for the wine bottle. There wasn't a drop left.

"So how'd Oliver look?" Tonna was sprawled on a deep, mocha leather couch, staring across at Marti, who was coiled in the matching chair. The gas fireplace crackled between them.

"Good," Marti said.

"Good or well?"

"Both. Your point is?"

"I was hoping he looked exhausted and miserable from missing you so much."

Marti leaned back and stared at the ceiling. "To be honest he looked rested and… happy."

"I'm sorry," Tonna said.

Marti laughed and then sighed. "Me too."

"But no talk of formalizing the split?"

"Not yet. I didn't bring *that* up."

"Don't you want some clarity? Guy up and leaves with no discussion and you just wait around? Eventually you'll need closure to move on."

"I'm not moving on. Oliver's the end of the line for me in the romance department."

"Please. You're thirty-six. I've had three boyfriends since I was your age."

Tonna was lowballing. She'd had at least five relationships since she landed in Dog Town four years ago. It helped that she met a lot of guys through her job, but there was no question that she had a pull over men. She was as welcoming and comfortable as her oversized leather furniture.

"Don't you want to, I don't know…"

"Settle down?" Tonna asked. "No, Mom, I don't."

"Did you ever?"

Tonna thought about it. "Maybe for a minute when I was in college. Guess I thought I had to. But once I started travelling the world, I realized I never wanted to be tied down." She ruffled Diva's fur. "This is the biggest commitment I've ever made."

Marti snorted. "You sold yourself a little short."

Raising the struggling dog, Tonna kissed her spikey head. "True that."

Marti didn't know much about Tonna's family. She'd never gone "home" in the time Marti had known her and if she did speak of her parents, her voice would harden. Further, while she claimed to be happy in Dorset Hills, Marti got the sense Tonna's suitcases were always handy in case she needed to make a quick exit. Maybe her new guy, Levi, would change all that.

After a few minutes of silence, Tonna said, "You should fight for Oliver."

Shifting in her chair, Marti said, "If he wants out, I won't hold him back."

"What if he just needs to know he matters? You're not exactly emotive, Marti. It wouldn't hurt you to give a little away."

Tonna was wrong about that. It would hurt a lot to chase Oliver. He should know he mattered—that no one else had since the day he walked into the coffee shop where she worked during grad school. Marti had been so nervous that she overfilled his cup and burned his hand. Luckily, he kept coming back and she gradually got over her paralyzed silence and started making him lattes with elaborate designs on top—leaves, feathers, and finally, a heart. Only much later did he admit he was lactose intolerant and had GI issues during their entire courtship. It was a sweet gesture that made her own stomach hurt now.

"Hank!" Marti leapt out of the chair. "Where is he?"

The distant crinkle should have alerted her earlier but she was out of practice. In the kitchen, Hank was surrounded by bits of chewed plastic. His white muzzle was now dark.

Tonna stared down at the mess. "That used to be a large bag of dried dates. It was behind the kettle on the counter."

"He's a magician," Marti said. The kettle had been gently nudged out of the way, instead of tipped. Hank had learned that stealth takes the cake. Literally.

"Is there anything he doesn't eat?"

Marti shook her head. "He lives by a code: eat first and ask questions later."

"Good thing dates aren't toxic for dogs. But they are high in fiber. Better get him outside before he explodes."

CHAPTER 7

*M*arti groaned as the click of nails on hardwood woke her again. She avoided looking at the clock on the bedside table. It was probably after three a.m., but what was the point in making it official?

Picking her way through the darkened house with practiced ease, she groaned. Hank had a terrible case of the runs and had already been out twice, where he raced around the snowy backyard as if pursued by demons. Each bout had required a gag-inducing clean-up of his fuzzy posterior, not to mention plucking snowballs off his legs. There were pools of melted snow all over the house.

If Oliver had set this up as a test, she was willing to concede defeat. The only thing that kept her from calling him on the spot was the knowledge that she'd been careless. From the start, Hank could not be left unattended in a room with anything chewable. In other words, any room. Despite their vigilance, he'd found opportunities to devour two pairs of sunglasses, three remotes, a phone, socks, a rubber glove, several shoes and boots, a length of garden hose, a basket of zucchini (basket included), a large frozen turkey, and innumerable toys rated "indestructible." It was

48

amazing that he'd only required surgery twice. Most foreign objects passed unscathed.

Hank pranced ahead of her to the back door, spirit unquenched. Round the clock diarrhea wasn't new or particularly stressful for him. He was as eager to go out at three as he had been at one and two a.m. Marti, on the other hand, rested her forehead against the cold glass of the door as he circled the yard. She saw Oliver's point now. When this had happened in the past, he'd always been the one to take care of it. Maybe she *had* taken him for granted.

She felt herself drifting a bit, remembering how nice it had felt to have Oliver slip back into bed and pull her close to chase away the chill. He'd joked that warming him up was the price she had to pay for staying in bed. One thing often led to another, and there was a wonderful, illicit feeling to those middle-of-the-night encounters.

A harsh screech shook her awake. Fumbling for the door handle, she went outside and across the porch in her slippers. The sleet of earlier had frozen into ice, lumpy with Hank's paw prints. The dog himself was out of sight, deep in the yard, she supposed. There was a stretch of tall trees close to the six-foot fence that shielded them from the ravine beyond.

"Hank?" More screeching. Not Hank's voice.

Her hand missed the railing and she fell down the last two steps, hitting her knee hard on the ice before falling onto her back. Flailing like a tipped-over turtle, she tried to get purchase on something, anything to right herself as the screeching doubled. Now, Hank's voice. Whatever he'd been giving, he was now getting back.

Adrenaline gave her the jolt she needed to flip and scramble to her feet. Running through the yard, she slipped again, this time landing in a reeking pile of dog poop. It was semi-frozen, obviously from their previous outing. Driven on by the yowling, she pushed herself to her feet again and wiped her hand on her bathrobe.

Now she was crying, warm tears dripping down cold cheeks. "Hank!"

There was silence ahead and she picked her way forward more carefully. It was dark back here. If they got out of this alive, these trees were coming down.

A rustle ahead stopped her. Hank hurtled out of the trees, whimpering. He jumped up on her, nearly toppling her a third time, but she clutched the trunk of a tree. Hank gave a great shake and dark drops splattered her robe. Blood.

Nonetheless, Hank turned to go back after whatever had attacked him.

Shouting, "No!" Marti lunged for his collar and dragged him, writhing, through the yard, up the stairs and inside.

"THAT'S QUITE A FILE," Dr. Benson said, scrolling through Hank's record on the computer screen.

Weak light streamed through the examination room's single window as the sun crept over the horizon. Marti had driven 40 minutes to the 24-hour clinic Oliver preferred. The costs were lower here, and with bills like Hank's it was better to burn some time and fuel.

All of Hank's bravado had disappeared now. He cowered against her as the vet perched on a low stool and wheeled toward him.

"You guys offer a points card?" Marti asked. Hank's wounds were still bleeding, but his eyes were fine and his low whine had tapered off. Once before he'd ended up with a raging infection from a bite hidden in thick fur, though, and Marti wasn't taking any chances.

The vet's smile was kind. His features were nice, but he looked like he never saw enough sun. "Racoon?" he asked.

"Probably," Marti said. "A coyote couldn't scale the fence."

"I thought Hank had settled down. Haven't seen him in months."

"He was away for a while. Financing vets out of state."

Picking through Hank's coat, Dr. Benson laughed. "Some dogs are just unlucky from the get-go."

"I'm the unlucky one. Hank just makes poor choices."

When he finished shaving and dressing the wounds, the vet stood. "He'll need to wear a cone for a few days so he doesn't lick. I'll send you home with some antibiotic ointment and—"

There was a ripping noise behind Marti. Hank had torn a hole into one of the huge bags of dog food heaped in the corner. Kibble spilled out onto the floor, and despite the deep gashes on his snout, Hank was gobbling the food up as fast as he could.

"I'm so sorry," Marti said. "Add that to my bill."

The vet laughed again as he pulled the bag of food out of reach. Marti held Hank back by his collar, but it was like wrestling a slippery pig.

"Care for a little advice?" he asked.

"If there's a zoo willing to take him, he's free."

Dr. Benson pointed to her wrist, which was swelling after her fall in the yard. "I bet there are bruises to go with that. People will think you've been beaten."

Marti sighed. "The ice adds a layer of complexity to Hank management."

"Well, I don't need to tell you that he's a high energy dog," he said. "One of the highest I've seen. He'll settle eventually, but in the meantime your best bet is intensive obedience training, combined with structured exercise."

"Structured?"

"Not at a dog park, where he could get even more excited. Play fetch. Take agility courses. Or let him run in the hills."

Marti sighed again. Taking Hank out in public would be a challenge. "His recall isn't great."

Leaning against the examination table, the vet thought for a moment. "This isn't a popular concept, but in Hank's case, a remote collar wouldn't be a bad idea."

"You mean, like a shock collar?"

"Like a shock collar," he said. "I believe there's a place for correction when a dog as big as Hank gets unruly. But please don't quote me on that."

"Of course not," Marti said. "But I couldn't shock my pup."

"Introduce it properly, and it might only have to be once. With benefits forever."

Never, Marti thought. No matter how poorly he behaved. "Even if I wanted to, shock collars are banned in Dorset Hills. Along with any other corrective tool."

Spinning back and forth on his stool, he pursed his lips. "I've heard about the new zero tolerance policy. Do you want to know how that's going to end?"

Not really, Marti thought. Not now.

Dr. Benson didn't wait for a response. "Some people will give away their pets at the first sign of trouble. Then the dog will become even more insecure and harder to manage for the next owner. Dogs like Hank could be labelled irreparable. Then what happens?"

"What?" Marti's voice was a whisper, and her fingers twirled deeper in Hank's lush coat.

"People will come to see me. They'll be so afraid of the dog ending up in a bad situation that they ask me to take care of it."

"Take care of it? How?"

He stopped spinning to meet Marti's eyes squarely. "Permanently, that's how. They'll be beautiful dogs, most of them rowdy youths like Hank. And I'll have to say no, because I don't do that here."

Marti breathed a sigh of relief. "Thank god."

"Then, they'll go somewhere else. Further into the countryside, where vets might eliminate a problem, if the owner tells the right story."

"No. That won't happen," Marti insisted.

"Not to Hank, I'm sure. You'll do the work to prevent it. But others may not have the wherewithal—the intelligence, the persistence, or the funds for a trainer."

"I take it you know about my new role," she said.

He nodded. "I was hoping to have a word with you, but I didn't expect the opportunity to come so soon."

"I'll take your input under advisement," she said. It sounded like bureaucratese, so she added, "Seriously."

"I know you will. It's just that sometimes politicians act rashly, without really thinking about the repercussions downstream. And 'No Bad Dogs' could be very bad for dogs, and then very bad for politicians. Mark my words."

"Got it," she said, putting on her coat. "You'll be hearing from me downstream."

"Hank will see to that," he said, with a wink.

CHAPTER 8

*T*he cold in the courtroom barely fazed Marti now. It seemed downright balmy after her late night adventure. A hot shower and a shot of bourbon had gotten her to the point where she could drop off to sleep again, and by then, it was only an hour till her alarm.

Now she stared down, bleary-eyed, at the people assembled on each side of the courtroom. Today's defendant was Delilah, a shaggy patchwork of fur that came together as a restless Old English sheepdog. She was swivelling left and right, trying to rise, while her owner continually pressed her butt down with a hushed, "Sit. Sit."

To speed the proceedings along, Marti said, "So the plaintiff, Mrs. Andrews, alleges that Delilah has been in her yard repeatedly over the past month."

"Once," said Delilah's owner, Paul Maxwell, a taciturn man of about 60. "Twice at most."

"More like a dozen times," said Noreen Andrews. "Every time I look out my window, this shaggy beast is circling my garage."

"Well, maybe if you didn't keep chickens in your garage, that wouldn't happen," Paul said. "I'm pretty sure it's against municipal bylaws."

"I don't know what you're talking about," Noreen said. "And anyway, your dog's a runner. Runners aren't allowed in Dorset Hills."

"Chickens?" Marti asked. "What kind of chickens?"

"The illegal kind," Paul said. "With feathers and beaks. Not the kind in the frozen food aisle."

"Fine, understood," Marti said. "What relevance does this have here?"

"It's relevant because I've heard something crowing when the sun comes up, and it's coming from the general direction of Noreen's garage."

"That's ridiculous. I've had a cold, that's all. You can't sue someone for having a cold, can you?"

"I'm not suing anyone," Paul said. "I'm the defendant. But someone in a glass chicken coop shouldn't throw stones."

"I'm sure Ms. Andrews isn't keeping chickens on her premises," Marti said. "It's against municipal bylaws."

"Exactly," Noreen said. She covered her mouth and coughed loudly.

"Doesn't sound like an illegal cock to me," Paul said.

"Mr. Maxwell!" Marti's voice layered on top of Noreen's shrill protest.

"I think we're getting away from the point," Noreen said. "Delilah has been in my yard, and every yard in between, more than a dozen times. She hops a five-foot fence like it was nothing."

"She could clear six if the chickens were actually *loose* in the yard," Paul said, grinning at Marti.

Shaking her head, Marti said, "Mr. Maxwell, we have no evidence of any chickens. But we do have several witnesses to Delilah's wandering ways."

"She's a runner," confirmed another woman in the seat behind Noreen. "I have photos."

"Can I have a week to gather evidence about the chickens?" Paul asked. "I believe I could produce a cock for the court. Or more likely a hen."

Marti pressed her fingers to her lips to suppress a smirk. "Please don't, Mr. Maxwell. The issue at hand is Delilah's wandering. Dogs need to be leashed at all times in Dorset Hills proper, unless they're confined in their own yards. If Delilah can leap tall fences in a single bound, you're going to have to increase security."

"Judge Marti," Noreen said. "The dog needs to be banned from Dorset Hills. Just like you banned Guido. Zero tolerance, remember?"

Marti shrank into her robes. "Delilah hasn't shown the slightest aggression from what I've heard. So, unless someone says otherwise—"

"No chickens were harmed in the making of this farce," Paul Maxwell said.

"I'm going to let Delilah off with a warning and a fine," Marti continued. "If I see the two of you here again, Mr. Maxwell, we'll be having a different conversation."

"How about the chickens?" Paul said.

Marti closed her eyes and took a deep breath. "This is canine court. I have no jurisdiction over fowl."

"Fine, so I'll take Ms. Andrews to chicken court," he said. "Who got cherrypicked for that job?"

"Thank you, we're adjourned," Marti said, rising and sweeping out of the room with a flourish of robes.

Back in her office, she closed the door and laughed. Then she called Tonna and they laughed some more.

A discreet knock silenced Marti. Cliff Whorley, bow-tied and mustachioed, spoke through a crack in the door. "Shall I call the meeting, Director?"

"Sure, Cliff." Marti dropped her phone in her bag. "Call me Marti, please."

Cliff was a former state trooper whose wife had convinced him to leave the force and move to Dorset Hills. As manager, he had run the former Canine Corrections Branch like a fiefdom for two years, until Marti was parachuted in as his new boss. Cliff could barely contain his disdain for Marti and she was so uncomfortable in his presence that she avoided him. Her key priority in the coming months would be winning over the tough ex-cop. For now, they'd settled on a brittle civility that probably fooled no one.

"Yes, Director, of course," he said, retreating to round people up.

It was the first day all the staff had been in the new office, and it was time for the official rallying call. Marti had been to enough of these meetings to know how it was done, but she wasn't looking forward to it. None of them had been at all welcoming.

She knew their job wasn't easy. Until Christmas, Dorset Hills citizens had raised concerns that the City was slow to follow up on complaints about dog infractions. The single investigator had struggled to keep up with the more serious complaints; it was often months before he got to the minor ones. By this time, fuses had sometimes become very short, and small issues escalated.

On top of that massive pile of poop, the volume of complaints had quadrupled since the introduction of the Tattle Tail hotline. Once people had the means to snitch privately, they took full advantage of it. Now the CCD was scrambling to staff-up to meet demand.

After removing her robes, she joined the staff in the boardroom, taking the closest seat to the door. Cliff nodded to the head of the table, and she reluctantly moved. "Hello, gentlemen," she said. "I've heard a lot about you, and I know Cliff has gathered a top-notch team. We have some big challenges ahead as a division, but at least I know we're well supported here."

Cliff cleared his throat. "Actually, Director, we're sorely understaffed at the moment. My team—er, *the* team—handles dozens of dog-related complaints per week. We don't have enough boots on the ground to stay ahead."

Marti looked around at the men. Two of them looked like brawny ex-cops, or security guards, and the others looked like typical bureaucrats. "Okay, I hear you. Draw up a business case, and we'll review the budget."

"Of course, Director. Just to let you know Mayor Bradshaw indicated there's room in the budget for two more investigators."

"Two? I know complaints are high now, Cliff, but that ought to drop when the novelty of the Tattle Tail hotline wears off. That's usually the pattern, right? We should probably monitor for a while before rushing into anything. The department has a lot of priorities right now."

Cliff's flush deepened and he straightened his already precise bow tie. "The mayor seemed to think two was a good number."

Marti read between the lines. Mayor Bradshaw had promised Cliff an increase in the size of his team to compensate for giving her the director role and demoting him to manager. If she fought him on this, he'd turn into an active enemy versus a passive one. Marti had never played games well in previous roles. She'd kept her head down and worked hard, but when it came to this sort of maneuvering, she was naive. That was why her appointment to this position was so strange.

"All right, Cliff," she said. "I'll leave this in your capable hands. May I suggest that we hire short-term at first?"

Cliff and his henchmen leaned forward as one. "The mayor never said contract, ma'am. It's impossible to get good people short-term."

Marti leaned back. "Understood. I'm sure there's room in the budget for that."

There was no point being stingy with the pilfered community

health funding, she figured. There was a good chance it would never be reallocated to its rightful portfolio anyway. Instead of watching every penny, as she'd initially intended, she'd use the money to help the dogs of Dorset Hills.

The good ones, of course, and the bad ones, even more.

CHAPTER 9

here was a neat little pile of mail on the porch when Marti got home. It had a light dusting of snow and was curling from dampness. Marti wondered why her typically conscientious mail carrier had chosen a January day to boycott the mail slot in her front door.

Brushing the snow off the pile of bills and magazines, she saw a large brown envelope that appeared to have been ravaged. There were tooth marks all over one end and so much of the envelope had been torn away that the statement of her investments was exposed for the mailman, at least, to see.

On the remains of the envelope was a note in blurred blue ink:

Sorry, Ms. Forrester. I tried to put the mail in the slot and something on the other side tore it up real bad. Either you got a Tasmanian Devil problem, or Hank's back. Let me know where you want me to leave the mail. P.S. I did not look at your bank stuff.

"Fantastic," Marti muttered, fighting her way past Hank into the house. Once your mailman knows you've got a bad dog, it's only a matter of time before the rest of the town hears about it. What would happen if the dog court judge got called up on charges? The mayor would have her head—or Hank's—on a platter.

She leashed Hank and took him into the yard, wincing as he smacked her shins with a plastic cone roughly the size of a satellite dish. He seemed subdued, but the cone of shame tended to take the spark out of a dog. Surely he'd be okay without it for an hour or two under strict supervision.

Marti removed the cone and gave him a sanctioned chew toy as she went through her files, made her lunch and chose her clothes for the next day. She firmly believed that the foundation of her success—such as it was—was good organizational skills. If she had a plan, and worked the plan, things usually fell into place.

Hank had thrown a wrench into the works, but Marti still had hope that with vigilance, she could get through this. The cuts and scratches would heal by the time Oliver returned and he'd be impressed that she'd survived unscathed. With panache, even. Then they could have the conversation they'd needed to have since before Hank even arrived. She was already rehearsing it in her head. Thinking on her feet had never been her strong suit. Her new job would likely change that, but not in two weeks.

Once they'd healed the rift, she and Oliver could tackle the problem of Hank together—this time with her full participation and accountability. They'd turn him into a good dog, and then she could focus on getting her career back on track.

By nine, she'd settled into bed with a book. Hank was on the rug nearby, his breathing deep and even. The book fell to her side as she watched him sleep. Even in his cone, he was a gorgeous beast. When he entered a dream cycle, his puffy white paws paddled and he made high-pitched woofing sounds. Perhaps he was chasing wildlife through dream meadows. It made her smile.

A few minutes after she turned out the light, there was a surprisingly gentle thud on the bed as Hank joined her. Stretching out on Oliver's side, he pressed his back against her and let out a huge sigh. Marti knew she should put him off the bed. This practice had stopped before Oliver left, because there wasn't a bed big enough for three when one was a massive heater. Judging by Hank's ease, however, she suspected Oliver had filled the gap in his bed the same way. Surrendering to the warmth, she decided to worry about the house rules in the morning and drifted away.

Within what seemed like minutes, but turned out to be hours, Marti was wide awake again. Hank was pacing across the hardwood with the warning tick-tick-tick of his claws. At the end of every turn, the plastic cone whacked her dresser.

"Not the runs again, buddy?" Swinging her legs over the side of the bed, she grabbed her robe. She'd applied a spot remover and run the robe through the heavy laundry cycle three times. The poop stains had come out, but the blood splatter had proven more resistant. At the front door, she hooked up Hank's leash. There was no way she'd risk another backyard fracas tonight. He'd have to do his business out front. She considered putting her coat on and decided not to bother. It was a cold, windy night and Hank tended to work quickly in adverse conditions.

The wind grabbed the robe instantly and lifted it in a Marilyn Monroe swirl that exposed her short, plaid nightshirt. She reached down to pull the edges of the robe together. Feeling slack in the lead, Hank plunged down the stairs, jerking the leash from her hand. Without so much as a look backwards, he took off, racing down the front walk and across the street.

"Hank!" she yelled, but all she could see was a flash of the white cone, and then nothing.

The wind carried off a string of profanity in Hank's general direction, and Marti followed as fast as her tread-less slippers allowed. She picked her way carefully from cleared patch to patch, very much aware of her bruises and stiffness from the previous night's exploits.

"Hank?" she called again, sweetening her tone. "Come!" In puppy class, the trainer had emphasised that responding to the "come" command should always be a pleasant experience no matter how angry the owner might be at that moment. Marti was furious, but also scared. There was no telling what Hank might get into next.

Relief came over her in a warm wave when she saw a bearlike form with white feet heading up the Galloways' driveway. A motion-activated light came on just in time to show Hank leaping at a tall trash bin. It came down with a crash, and the contents spilled out.

"Hank!" There was no honey in Marti's tone as she bellowed at him now. It didn't matter. Whatever was in that bin would have greater allure than anything she could offer.

By the time she reached him, Hank had tossed aside a week's worth of trash and torn into a bag to reach the carcass of a Christmas turkey. He had already broken it into pieces and was crunching the bones, head tipped back and eyes closed in bliss.

"Drop it!" she yelled.

Hank's eyes popped open and he chewed faster. When she came toward him, he turned away, wolfing down the bones as fast as he could.

Grabbing him from behind, she groaned as her wrist gave a savage twinge. But knowing frozen cooked turkey bones could tear open Hank's intestines made her forge on. Climbing astride, she clamped down with her knees and pried open his jaws. One by one she pried out the bones. Then she took his leash and looped it over the fenccpost on the other side of the driveway.

Hank whined as she started putting the trash back into the bin, numb fingers making it slow work.

"Ssssh," she hissed, plucking wrappers and tissues off the driveway. Hank strained at the leash, and when she picked up the last bag, gave a booming bark. He didn't bark often—that was one of his better traits—but when he did, you knew it.

The front door opened, framing Ada Galloway, her wiry gray

hair standing on end. Ada's mouth dropped open when she saw Marti in the pool of light on the driveway.

Cracking open the screen door, she said, "Marti Forester! Whatever are you doing?"

It seemed perfectly obvious to Marti: she was picking through her neighbor's trash on a frigid night wearing only a stained housecoat and slippers. The real question was *why*, and she hoped she could escape before being asked. Ada was a lifer in Dorset Hills—a notorious gossip, and no friend of dogs.

"I'm so sorry, Mrs. Galloway," she said, through chattering teeth.

"Ada." Mrs. Galloway corrected her automatically as she stepped out onto the porch. She was wearing a filmy blue night-gown that was surprisingly sexy for a widow closing in on 70. More power to her, Marti thought.

"It's cold, Ada, stay inside," she said. "I'm just cleaning up after a little accident."

Ada leaned over the railing, revealing more than Marti cared to see. "Oh! Hank's back. Well, that explains everything."

Hank had been well known around the neighbourhood, and Oliver often had to turn on his charm to smooth the waters. Marti had been grateful cold weather had limited encounters with people who were curious about her status with her husband. She could count the prying questions on one hand, and that was unusual.

"I'll be done in a minute," she said. "Please go back inside."

But Ada's nosiness was able to withstand the frigid air. "So, Oliver's back?"

"He asked after you," Marti said. Working in the political realm was teaching her the fine art of avoiding a question without being rude.

Ada smiled. "He's a lovely man. I'm glad you two have worked things out."

"His parents are doing well, and it's nice he was able to leave them for a bit." Marti looked down just in time to see Hank suck in a burrito wrapper. "Leave it," she said, but it was already gone.

"Hank's gorgeous," Ada said. "But I see he still keeps you hopping."

"That he does. Literally." She bounced up and down to get the blood flowing.

"Marti, I insist you leave that and come inside for a moment. It'll be fine till the morning."

"No, it won't. There was a racoon around last night. Tore Hank up a bit."

"Around four? I thought I heard screaming."

Marti nodded, using one bare knee to nudge Hank away from the green garbage bag she was holding aloft. "Leave it," she repeated.

Darting around her leg, he sank his teeth into the bag and with a skilful twist, tore it open. The contents spilled onto the driveway. Hank grabbed something long and dark and started to back away with his treasure. Marti leaned over quickly and grabbed the other end.

Then she screamed.

"Oh my god, it's fur!" Her first thought was that it was a stuffed animal, but the object was hard and stiff and... formerly alive.

Ada ran down the stairs in bare feet. "Leave it. Leave it!"

Her voice had the ring of authority and Hank and Marti both dropped the furry object.

Bending, Ada grabbed it and shoved it back in the bag. When Hank leaned in, she rapped him smartly on the nose. Undeterred, he lunged again and grasped what appeared to be a tail. Ada dropped the bag and pulled back. The two had a tug of war.

"What is it?" Marti asked, as the leash slipped from her hand.

"Never mind," Ada snapped.

That wasn't the only thing that snapped. Hank gave his swift left-right head twist and ended up with the tail. He pranced toward Marti, brandishing the trophy. Marti now saw the stripes. It was indeed a tail, and it had likely belonged to a grey tabby she'd seen flitting around the neighbourhood.

"Oh no, poor kitty," Marti said. "Did it freeze to death?"

Nodding grimly, Ada stuffed the rest of the cat's body back into the bag. "Found it in my back yard."

"How sad." Marti noticed that Ada was using unnecessary force on the frozen remains. She must be broken up about it.

"Terribly." Ada let the bag fall and turned suddenly to Hank. "You drop that right now."

Hank did as he was told for a change and Ada picked up the tail.

"I'm so sorry, Ada." Marti clutched her robe to her neck, shivering in great wracking spasms.

"Go home and warm up. You're going to catch your death… I mean, catch cold." Ada seemed flustered, but it was no wonder really, when she'd been awoken to find someone picking over the bodies in her trash.

Marti started down the driveway, pulling Hank behind her.

"Marti?" Ada called after her.

Turning, Marti took in the odd tableau. Mrs. Galloway was standing barefoot and barely dressed in a pool of light, holding a cat's tail in one hand. She looked vulnerable, yet somehow defiant. "Yes, Ada?"

"I'd appreciate it if you didn't mention any of this."

"Of course not."

"And say hello to Oliver for me."

"I will."

Ada hastened to stuff the cat tail into the bag, and Marti hobbled back up the street, wondering if she'd ever feel her toes again.

CHAPTER 10

*M*arti's kitchen seemed about half the size when Cori Hogan strode into the room. It was an optical illusion. The kitchen was actually quite spacious, and Cori was no more than five-foot-three, with a wiry build, delicate features, and fine brown hair tied back in a wispy ponytail. She looked like a sharp-eyed sparrow. Or perhaps a small bird of prey.

"Now that," Cori said, in a surprisingly husky voice, "is a beautiful dog."

"I'll tell my friend you said so."

Kneeling beside Hank, Cori let him lick her face. "Don't bother."

"Pardon me?"

"Pretending that Hank isn't yours." Cori didn't even look up at Marti.

"Excuse me, but—"

Cori interrupted. "Hank's notorious in Dorset Hills."

"Notorious?" Marti didn't like the sound of that.

"Trainers have a grapevine, and Hank's reputation precedes him."

Since Hank had enjoyed the services of not one but four

different trainers in his early months, it wasn't shocking that word had spread. No doubt they'd consoled each other with tales of his intractability.

"Don't you guys have some sort of professional code?" Marti asked.

Cori stood up and shrugged. "War stories. I was hoping I'd get a chance at Hank one day, and then he disappeared. Figured you'd sent him back to his breeder."

"Look, Cori." Marti tried to sound dignified. "This probably isn't going to work out. I assumed—wrongly it would seem—that our dealings would be private."

"Relax," Cori said. "I won't say a word. I understand your situation completely."

"My... situation?"

"You're the judge in canine court. And Hank's a bear-sized blot on your reputation."

Cori chuckled as she sized Hank up. He sized her up in return, sitting pretty, with his head cocked.

Heat flooded Marti's face. Who did this woman think she was, anyway? It was hard to believe Tonna thought so highly of her.

"Okay, this was definitely a bad idea," Marti said. "I appreciate your coming out, but I'll handle this on my own."

"Up to you," Cori said. "But word really gets around in this town."

"Is that a threat?"

"Of course not," Cori said. "Jeez, you're wound pretty tight. I'm just making an observation about Dorset Hills. I'm as much a victim of the gossip as you are. Do you think it's easy being in dog rescue right now?"

Marti supposed not. If the veterinarian was right, people would be abandoning ill-behaved dogs right, left and center in the No Bad Dogs regime. But it wouldn't be appropriate for her to comment. Instead she raised her hands helplessly. "What could we do with this guy in a week or so anyway?"

"Lots, actually. And it'd be good for you, too."

Marti leaned back against the counter and crossed her arms. "You can tell that already."

Cori leaned against the fridge and mirrored Marti's pose. "I'll tell you what I see. If I'm right, we'll do some intensive training with Hank. If I'm wrong, I'm gone. The only condition is that you've got to be honest. Deal?"

Eying her warily, Marti nodded. "Okay."

Cori pushed off the fridge and circled Hank. He sidled away from her and onto Marti's feet. Sensing his anxiety, Marti reached down and stroked his soft ears. He leaned into her hand.

"Uh-huh," Cori said. "Just as I thought."

"What?"

Pointing at Marti's feet, she said, "He's parked on there like he owns you. Then, when he showed a bit of anxiety, you immediately reassured him. I'm guessing he sleeps in your bed, too."

"Not all the time."

"At his convenience, no doubt."

It was true. Hank only got down when he was too hot. Otherwise, he took up more than his share of the queen-sized bed. In the old days, Oliver had gotten the dog's back, and Marti the paws. Often she'd sensed Hank was trying to push her right out.

"Many people sleep with their dogs, if not most," Marti said.

"And many, if not most, have problem dogs. And some have problems with their marriage."

Marti suppressed a flinch, but Cori's eyes widened slightly. No doubt the trainer was astute at reading both human and canine body language.

"Sorry," Cori said. "I had no idea that— I mean, I'm not known for my tact. I thought your husband was just away."

"He is." Marti forced a smile. "But that doesn't mean Hank hasn't caused tension."

Cori nodded. "It's inevitable. So this is the perfect window. It's much harder to get two people to change than just one."

"What could we accomplish in so little time?"

"Miracles. I mean, Hank won't pass the Canine Good Citizenship Award anytime soon, but you'd be surprised what a few subtle changes can do." Cori took a step toward Hank and he tried to push backwards between Marti's knees. "See that? He's already nervous, knowing the cavalry's in town. You ready for the challenge?"

"Yeah, I think so." This felt like a now-or-never opportunity to turn things around. Not just for her job, but for her marriage. If Oliver took Hank away again, they'd probably be gone for good this time.

"Okay, the first thing you've got to do is realize you're pack leader. And then you've got to start acting like it."

Marti had heard that before, but no one had clarified the key element. "How?"

"I'll give you some simple rules to live by," Cori said. "First, no excuses. You created this problem, you own it."

"Wait a second. This dog was difficult from the day he arrived. Bernese mountain dogs are stubborn. It's his breed."

Covering her ears, Cori continued, "Excuses! Second, this is a dog, not a furry child. That means no bed, no couch, no chair by the fire. Four paws on the floor at all times. Third, you implement the NILF program—Nothing in Life is Free. What Hank wants, he works for." Leaning over, she felt his well-padded torso. "He's treat motivated. That's in your favor."

"He'll eat anything that isn't nailed down," Marti said. "And some things that are."

"I assume you've never crated him?" Cori said.

"He doesn't like to be confined."

"Excuses!"

"You asked," Marti said.

"It was a rhetorical question. I know a dog that's ruled the roost from the second we sniff each other. And this one's had too much freedom since the day he left his designer breeder."

Backing out from under Hank's feet, Marti said, "There's no need to get snarky."

Cori looked up at Marti with fierce brown eyes. "I'm not here to be nice. Or to make money, believe it or not. I'm here for the dog, Marti. I see dogs like Hank get surrendered to rescues all the time, and some never recover."

"I would never abandon Hank," Marti said.

"Sure sounded like it when you called from Tonna's the other night."

Busted. "That was temporary. While my husband is away."

"Wow, you really are attached to your excuses," Cori said.

"Wow, you really are harsh." Marti picked up an apple from the counter just to keep her hands busy. What she really wanted to do was pitch it at Cori's smug face.

"If I'm harsh, it's because Dorset Hills is making me that way. This No Bad Dogs mandate is breaking my heart. Thanks to people like you, dogs like Hank get no second chances."

"Like me? I'm not an elected official. I'm a bureaucrat." But Marti realized that excuse didn't fly, either. She'd been appointed to a quasi-political role. Now, she was just a different kind of yes-woman.

Cori studied her as keenly as she had Hank. "I can tell you're getting a whiff of the bullshit."

"You'd better go," Marti said. "This isn't working out."

"That's my line," Cori said, shoving her arms into her coat. "If you're not committed, Hank will sense it, and training won't stick. Believe it or not, he wants to trust you and please you. Don't let him down again."

Marti set the apple on the counter and followed Cori to the front door. Hank nuzzled the trainer's ear while she pulled on her boots. Now that she was leaving, it was safe to show interest.

"Take it easy on the mailman, bud," she said, giving his ear a friendly tug. Looking up, she met Marti's glare with a grin. "Posties have a grapevine, too."

"Sometimes I hate this…" Marti let her sentence trail off.

"Bullshit town." Cori finished her sentence for her.

"That's not what I was—" Hank stopped the excuses by jumping up and bouncing off her hip.

"So, I'm going to leave January eleventh open for you," Cori said. "Seven p.m. In the meantime, I'll be sending daily lessons you can follow on your own. You'll need to put in at least an hour's work on training morning and night."

"Two hours? Who has two hours for training?"

"Someone who loves her dog?"

Marti finally snapped. "Having an ill-behaved dog doesn't mean you don't love him."

"No, but it does mean you don't love them the right way. And that can be corrected… without resorting to tranquillizers, or shock collars, or any other bogus excuses you've come up with for not doing your work."

"I can't even—"

"Come up with one more excuse."

"I hate people who interrupt all the time," Marti said.

"Training Hank will help you speak with more authority. You've got to learn when to say no, and mean it."

"No. And I mean it."

With her hand on the doorknob, Cori paused. "Look, I hate giving you one more excuse, but I want you to know you're not alone."

"Meaning?"

"A lot of people are soft on their dogs, but especially women. Most of us aren't brought up to be confident leaders. I don't know about you, but I had to find my voice as an adult."

That comment hit home. As much as she'd loved him, Marti's dad had been the "children should be seen and not heard" type. Meanwhile, her mom had been a model of self-restraint, and allowed no pets in the house. It seemed that as far as dog rearing went, she'd been set up for failure.

"Interesting observation, Cori," she said. "Food for thought."

"More food for thought: You owe it to yourself and Hank to give this another try. So sleep on it." Opening the door, Cori slipped out. "Just make sure Hank's got—"

"Four on the floor. I know."

Cori poked her gloved hand back in and gave Marti the thumbs-up.

Marti didn't need to sleep on it. It only took about a minute for her to realize that Cori was right. She opened the door to tell her so, but Cori was already jogging up the street to her old van. No one liked parking on Marti's steep driveway.

"Damn it," Marti said, turning. "*Hank!*"

Hank had his head in the laundry basket she'd left on the floor by the stairs. Backing away, he hauled on a hot pink bra. One end was caught between the plastic slats, and the basket slid along the floor with Hank as he hit reverse.

"Leave it," she said. "Drop it. Drop. Drop. Drop!"

Hank did his signature left-right head swivel and as usual it worked magic. The basket released the bra's clasp and with a flashy snap, Hank was off. Marti made a grab for him, but he dodged around her and out the open front door. He stopped at the end of the driveway to make sure she was going to pursue, and when he saw her pulling on her boots, he was off again.

This time, Marti gathered her parka, mittens, and scarf before starting out. Her fingers and toes still tingled from last night and she wasn't going to risk frostbite.

Hank was out of sight when she reached the end of the driveway. She considered getting in the car to follow, but on foot, she could see his paw prints clearly in the light snow that had fallen in the past hour. It would be easier to track him this way.

She'd expected him to cross at the Galloway house, but he

continued on. His trail wove back and forth, as if he were drunk. Every so often, the prints would stop and double up. There was a swish in the snow, where he dragged the bra. *A bra angel*, she thought. In one spot, she could see two faint depressions in the snow where he'd actually dropped the bra. *An angel with a C-cup*. At least her favourite bra was seeing some action. It had been a long time since she'd seen any herself. She fought off a giggle and sighed instead.

Hank travelled two blocks before taking a hard right down a path through a small ravine. The snow was still blowing, so Marti yanked up her hood and pulled her scarf over her face.

On the other side, she emerged in the parking lot of a drug store she'd visited often with Hank. It was closed now, and aside from a lone car under a film of snow, the lot was empty.

Hank wasn't hard to find. Naturally, he was circling the dumpster looking for scraps. Her bra sat in a lonely heap, but the second Hank saw Marti, he grabbed it again. Then he danced in front of her, dangling the bra just out of reach. Reach she did, however. Again and again, she grabbed for it, despite knowing that "keep-away" was a game Hank always won.

When it looked like she was giving up, he came a little closer, just enough to give her hope, and then flitted away. He gave the bra a flamboyant death shake and pranced sideways like a dressage horse. The lumbering bear had some smooth moves when he was in the mood.

They circled the parking lot three times and Marti only managed to grab the bra once before it got snapped away. Finally, she called it.

"Fine, Hank, it's yours," she mumbled through her scarf.

The fabric was shredding anyway. This bra was a goner. Maybe Oliver would be sad to hear of its passing, since it was the first of many he'd chosen for her. If lingerie came back on their relationship menu, he could replace it.

"I'm going home, you idiot." Relenting, she added, "Come, Hank."

Marti walked out of the parking lot, back through the ravine, and up her street. It was a risky strategy, but all she could come up with at the moment.

Pushing her hood back slightly, she could see that Hank was following. He noticed the movement, and slowed to a stop, recalibrating. For once, Marti decided to trust her gut and carried on.

Finally, they reached the driveway and Hank charged past her and up the stairs. Dropping the slobbery, mangled bra on the welcome mat, he planted his butt and grinned at her. As far as he was concerned, this had been the best game ever.

Stepping over the bra, she went inside. Hank followed quickly, perhaps anticipating the slam that came as soon as his white-tipped tail cleared the doorway.

Ⓜarti hoped she looked imposing with a down vest under her robes, rather than just fat. She was fed up with being cold. After spending hours outside with Hank every night, she wasn't going to freeze in this courtroom by day.

There was only one hearing scheduled, for which she was grateful. They were incredibly draining, and she craved a few hours in her own office. It was time to learn more about what the Canine Corrections team did, and ideally, how they could do things differently. Further, Marti wanted to go over the new regulations again, this time with a fine-tooth comb. When policy happened on the fly, there were always loopholes, intended or otherwise. If there was room for discretion, she intended to find it.

The complainants had been in the courtroom even before Marti arrived, perched on their folding chairs. Following the usual pattern, the defendants trailed in moments before the hearing was to begin. Meanwhile, Marti scanned their submissions once more.

In the middle of the front row, on the defendants' side, sat Cori Hogan. She raised her hand, and Marti saw that the middle finger of the otherwise black glove was fluorescent orange. She'd done some checking after Cori's visit and confirmed that she was part of the so-called Rescue Mafia the mayor had mentioned. Apparently Cori wasn't afraid to flip the bird to anyone, even in a so-called courtroom.

"Ms. Hogan," Marti said. "I don't see your name in the submissions."

"I'm a witness for the accused, Judge."

The accused in question was a sleek and regal-looking Weimaraner appropriately named King. The dog had allegedly taken an instant dislike to the complainant, Mildred Mumford, who had been collecting door-to-door for a cancer charity. Mrs. Mumford, in her seventies, had fled at the first growl with King in pursuit. When she couldn't open the gate, Mrs. Mumford had attempted to scale it. Needless to say, that had not gone well.

Marti looked at King's owners, the Aguilars, a seemingly mild-mannered couple. Indeed, she had seen Mrs. Aguilar behind the desk of the Main Street library on the few occasions she'd borrowed a book. "Witnesses are to be identified in advance submissions," Marti said. "As stipulated in regulation."

Mr. Aguilar rose. "Judge, I understand that subsection 6.5 of the guidelines states that Canine Corrections authorities have discretion in administering the regulation. I would interpret that to mean you can choose to allow a character witness."

He sat down abruptly, looking relieved. His speech had sounded rehearsed, and Cori was wearing a smug smile. She had obviously sized up the loopholes before Marti could and decided to see if she could fit through them. Now it was on Marti to decide how she wanted to interpret the regulations, and potentially set a precedent.

She pondered for a moment. The Aguilars would have the right to appeal, and would be shot down at a higher level, no question about that. Marti could stick to the regulations and avoid getting snagged by the loopholes. But now was probably as good a time as any to start making tough decisions. After all, she'd had to pry a frozen pink bra off her porch that morning with a dinner knife. Life in Dog Town was getting more complicated every day.

"I'll allow the witness," she said. "Unless the complainant has a strident objection."

Mildred Mumford shrugged, no doubt assuming the case was open and shut anyway. There couldn't be a loophole big enough for a Weimaraner chasing an old lady collecting for cancer.

Indeed, Mrs. Mumford described the incident quickly and efficiently. Mr. Aguilar had opened the door to hand her a 20-dollar bill. King had pushed past him, and chased Mrs. Mumford down the walk.

"May I speak, your honor?" Cori said.

"Were you there at the time of the incident, Ms. Hogan?" Marti asked.

"I was not. But I saw a photo in the paper and noticed that Mrs. Mumford was wearing a fur coat. Weimaraners are known for their high prey drive, and I believe that when she started running, he perceived her as—"

"Dinner?" Marti interrupted. "People should be allowed to wear whatever coat they want in January without being taken down like a seal on an ice floe." She caught herself and added, "Sorry, Mrs. Mumford."

The old woman waved the apology away.

Cori continued. "I would argue that fur coats are never appropriate, Judge. But my point is that by running, Mrs. Mumford turned herself into prey."

Mrs. Mumford stood up and turned to Cori. "So I was just supposed to stand there and get tackled? Young lady, I am seventy-two years old."

"I'm sorry, ma'am," Cori said. She raised both hands, with their two neon knit middle fingers. "I'm just trying to explain it from the dog's point of view. He was perfectly calm until you started running. And as I understand it, when you were climbing the fence, he went for the coat, although your leg was more readily available."

"He savaged a chinchilla coat that belonged to my mother," Mrs. Mumford said. "I would have preferred he'd gone for my leg."

There was a titter from the audience on both sides.

"Obviously, neither is appropriate," Marti said. "Any kind of aggression by a dog toward a person is prohibited in Dorset Hills."

Cori raised her hand again. "That's exactly my point, Judge. King didn't aggress toward a person, but an inanimate object. I've been unable to find reference to chinchilla coats in the new regulation. Therefore, I believe there is discretion to dismiss this case."

There was an uproar from Mrs. Mumford's side of the room. Her son started shouting, but Marti couldn't hear what he was saying, because Cori was giving it back. This time, Marti reached easily for the gavel and brought it down hard. She allowed everyone to settle into their seats before speaking.

"Look, Ms. Hogan, I appreciate your presenting the dog's-eye view. But King's teeth could very easily have pierced the coat and given Mrs. Mumford a nasty bite."

"The coat was in shreds," Mrs. Mumford confirmed.

Cori bobbed up again. "He didn't get near her skin and he could have. He exercised restraint in excitement."

"I was stuck on that fence until the owner got the dog inside and then helped me down," Mrs. Mumford says. "Take a moment and imagine that. It was terrifying."

"I'm sure it was." Cori looked like she was indeed imagining it, because she was clearly fighting a grin. "But you must admit that the owners are kind people. Once they got you down, they gave another hundred dollars to the cancer charity."

"A buy-off," Mrs. Mumford said.

"And they offered to pay for your coat," Cori added.

"It's priceless."

Cori pressed on. "What if you could settle on a price?"

Again the gavel banged down. "Ms. Hogan, sit. I'm presiding over this courtroom."

Mrs. Mumford raised her hand. "Judge, I'm willing to hear Mr. Aguilar's offer."

Marti sighed and shook her finger at Cori. "Mr. Aguilar, we'll hear you on the matter of the coat."

Mr. Aguilar rose. "I did some research and a coat of this vintage could be worth up to a thousand dollars."

"Make it twelve hundred, and another three hundred to the cancer fund," Mrs. Mumford, said, without missing a beat.

Cori jumped to her feet. "Done."

For the second time in less that 24 hours, Marti felt the urge to thump Cori—someone she'd just met. There was something about the trainer that caused aggression in humans, even if it reduced it in dogs. "I will decide what's 'done,'" she said.

"Your honor, I'm satisfied," Mrs. Mumford said. "This young lady is probably right that I shouldn't have run. And no one my age should be climbing a fence. I guess I should have used more common sense."

Marti had been had and she knew it. Cori had used the courtroom to negotiate a settlement. Well, there was still room for discretion, and Marti intended to use it.

"It's wonderful that you're so accommodating now, Mrs. Mumford. Unfortunately, the court doesn't agree that a monetary settlement is sufficient to address the issue of a dog attacking someone, whether or not the coat was the actual target."

Both sides erupted, intent on maintaining their negotiated peace.

Bang bang! The gavel felt like it was part of Marti's hand now. If she banged it at just the right spot, with just the right force, she could make the bust of Edgar Bolton, Dorset Hills' founder, tremble on its stand at the back of the room.

"Enough," she said. "I will honor your settlement. However, the court also issues a two-hundred-dollar fine, and sentences King to three months of obedience training. I'll see you back here then for follow up. If I'm not satisfied at that point, the penalty will be much stiffer."

Cori leapt to her feet. "But Judge—"

Bang!

"I'm using my discretion, Ms. Hogan. Court adjourned."

CHAPTER 12

*M*arti retreated to her office and closed her door. She wouldn't be at all surprised if the mayor summoned her to City Hall. The *Expositor* reporter, Leslie Longland, had materialized out of nowhere and was interviewing people as they left the courtroom. The type of story she wrote would probably be a good indication of how big her crush was on the mayor. Marti guessed it was big enough; she'd never seen a better-dressed newshound.

Outside her office, most of the cubicles were empty. Marti had a feeling she should know where everyone was, but she needed a moment to decompress anyway. Only the young guy with auburn hair was at his desk. She couldn't remember his name, but knew his job was to triage complaints as they came in. It wasn't easy being on the front lines in the new No Bad Dogs regime.

After a few blissful moments of peace, there was a knock at the door.

"Morning, Judge," Cliff said, poking his head in. His complexion had always been ruddy, but it had become positively florid since being passed over for her post. Marti supposed she'd know they had reached a détente when his color ebbed.

"Morning, Cliff," she said. She had given up urging him to call her Marti. It was his little protest. He alternated between "Judge" and "Director" at whim.

"You'll meet us in the boardroom?" he asked.

"Sure. For what?"

Cliff's furrowed brow folded in on itself. "The interviews, Judge. For the canine investigators."

"Already?" They'd only discussed it two days ago. How could they have run a competition so fast? "I mean, of course. Be right there."

"Good," Cliff said, although he looked disappointed. She knew he wanted her to be a silent figurehead, but the mayor had made her accountable for all decisions made at the CCD. After what happened in court earlier, it might be better to stay on top of things, even the hiring of dog "cops."

"Just give me a couple of minutes," she said.

After he left, she slumped in her chair and hid behind the computer monitor. This job had dragged her right out of her comfort zone of research, policy papers and implementation plans, and thrown her into the spotlight. Perhaps she would appreciate this growth opportunity somewhere down the line, but not today.

Digging her phone out of her purse, she looked at it and sighed. She didn't want to admit how often she checked for messages from Oliver. She'd didn't expect him to care about how she was doing, but it seemed strange that he didn't reach out about Hank. He had to know it wouldn't be an easy adjustment for the dog, and it wasn't like Oliver to be callous. At least, with the dog. He had no trouble callously walking away from her. Maybe she didn't know him that well after all.

There was a new e-mail with an unknown sender and the subject line, "This is hilarious." Spam, she figured, but she could certainly use some hilarity. She opened the e-mail and read the note. "You'll love this video. Sincerely, DogFraudBuster."

DogFraudBuster? Now she was really curious.

Clicking on the link, she saw a still shot of someone in a parka playing tug-of-war with a large black-and-white dog. Stretched out between them was a pink toy.

It took five-six-seven clicks before Marti could get the video to play. The 70-second snippet captured the full spectrum of the encounter: Hank snapping the bra out of her hand, prancing away and giving it the death shake, and taunting her just out of reach as she grabbed for it, again and again. The video ended with her walking away in a huff, and Hank staring after her, before reluctantly following. The drugstore store sign was visible, along with the dumpster.

Marti watched it over and over. Thanks to the parka, hood and scarf, she was probably unrecognizable. Hank, on the other hand, showed his full colors, and he was a very distinctive dog. Viewers might confuse him in the dim video for a full Bernese, perhaps.

If she was lucky, it was possible that no one other than DogFraudBuster would put two and two together and link the dog court judge with this unruly mutt. But he or she knew full well it was her and could at any time send it to the mayor, or post it on social media. Might have already, come to think of it.

A knock on the door made her jump. The door opened a crack to reveal Cliff's moustache again. "Judge, we're waiting," he said.

"Coming." She dropped the phone back into her purse and slammed the drawer closed.

MARTI SUSPECTED Cliff had staged the interviews so that the only female candidate came last. He'd clearly counted on the three men who'd warmed the chair across the boardroom table to impress. The only problem was that they were nearly indistinguishable. All were young and earnest aspiring cops who hadn't yet made it onto the police force. They were settling on Canine Corrections as a way to get some law enforcement experience and would likely be long gone when a real cop position opened up. All had performed well on the screening interviews and aptitude tests. And all gave similar answers to complex scenarios the interviewers presented. All gave the canned message about loving dogs —but only well-behaved dogs.

None of them actually owned a dog.

When Kinney Butterfield slid into the hot seat, Marti knew right away that Cliff was throwing her a bone, so to speak. He didn't want to leave an opening for complaints about discrimination, but at the same time, he didn't want a woman to get the job.

Kinney was probably in her early thirties, but she looked older. Or at least looked tired. Her blue eyes were bloodshot and puffy. Marti knew how hard it was to hide a night of tears past a certain age. She'd not had much success with ice cubes, teabags or cucumber slices. And she'd tried all of them this week.

Cliff ran through the interview questions, and where the male candidates had been confident and decisive, Kinney was slower, and more thoughtful. Where the men were black and white, she saw gray area. As a former social worker, Marti supposed it came with the territory.

When Cliff exhausted his questions, Marti asked, "Why do you want this job, Kinney? The City has a social worker position posted and you obviously have the experience."

Kinney folded and refolded her hands before answering. "I need a change," she said, simply. "Social work can be very draining."

"Helping dogs and dog owners can be draining, too," Marti said.

"Oh, I know." Kinney smiled for the first time. "Dog people are crazy."

Marti laughed. "They can be. But we live in Dog Town. That's our business."

Cliff didn't like Marti going off script. "This job can be hard, physical work," he said. "Pursuing runaways, climbing fences, intervening in dogfights, you name it."

Kinney's eyes dropped ever so briefly to Cliff's comfortable paunch before saying, "Of course. I'm really fit from roller derby."

"Roller derby?" His moustache twitched in disgust. "There's no roller derby in Dorset Hills."

"Sometimes Pemsville offers what Dorset Hills can't," Kinney said.

Marti liked Kinney better by the moment. She wasn't afraid of Cliff, and she had a sense of humor.

"Do you have a dog, Kinney?" she asked.

Kinney's lower lip trembled and her eyes filled. "I did, until last week. My golden retriever died of cancer."

"I'm so sorry," Marti said, and her own eyes filled.

"Thank you," Kinney said. "It took me four years to get him trained properly and then he died at six. I feel gutted… and ripped off."

Cliff shifted in his chair. "Goldens are the easiest dogs to train."

"Maybe. Not for me," Kinney said. "But he got his Canine Good Citizenship award last year."

"Your persistence paid off," Marti said. Cliff's eyebrows and moustache were all twitching erratically, but Marti ignored them. "You know, I think we need people like you who understand the nuances of the dog world, Kinney. You're hired."

Kinney ran around the boardroom table and grabbed Marti in a half-hug.

Cliff actually gasped. "Sit down, Ms. Butterfield. We do not do that here."

"Oh, Cliff," Marti said. "Didn't you get the memo? Friday is hug day, here at the CCD."

Kinney opened her arms toward Cliff and he backed slowly

out of the room, muttering something about telling the mayor, this being "highly irregular."

"Come and see me when you've signed the paperwork, Kinney," Marti said. "I have a project for you. And it's not without risk."

Kinney smiled and said, "Game on."

CHAPTER 13

On the bright side, Cliff hadn't had a heart attack, Marti thought, pressing hard on the gas pedal as she left the city the next morning. It had seemed touch and go there for a few minutes, as his color intensified to a perilous puce. Marti had ignored protocol, which required that the trio of interviewers discuss and agree on candidates after the process ended. Technically, her colleagues could have banded together and vetoed her decision to hire Kinney. Cliff had been somewhat mollified to hear that the budget allowed them to hire another one of his waxwork cop wannabes as well. But there was a greater reward for Cliff: now, he had something concrete to use against her with the mayor.

Marti had gone rogue. She was making impulsive decisions. That was probably enough to make Cliff order judicial robes in a bigger size, with room for a bow tie. Well, at the moment, Marti didn't care. If Cliff wanted the job so much, she'd pass the gavel to him and request a demotion. There was always some all-work, no-glory project in need of a good civil servant.

Hank rested his head on her shoulder, leaving a patch of slobber on her parka. She didn't think he was picking up on her mood. He just loved car rides—any ride, anywhere. Since he wasn't allowed in the front, he typically pushed as much of his white bib between the seats as he possibly could. If he had opposable thumbs, he'd fight her for the wheel.

"I got a surprise for you, buddy," she said, taking the next exit off the highway. Hank licked her ear, and she swatted him away. "Eww."

A few turns later, they were on a narrow road heading up the highest hills in the area. The scenery was breathtakingly beautiful in summer. In January, with the trees raising bare arms to an overcast sky, it was still breathtaking but in a terrifying way as one patch of ice could spell a driver's undoing.

Marti was practically hyperventilating as she drove under a massive arch and into the parking lot of the Hilltop Inn. They could have been more original with the name, she thought, pulling into a space near the front entrance. The place was rustic, but nice enough.

The desk clerk directed Marti to a cabin behind the main lodge. Collecting Hank from the car, she led him along a shovelled path, between shoulder-high snow banks. They stopped in front of cabin number three, and Marti knocked on the door.

Oliver was wearing his torn navy blue sweatpants and an even rattier T-shirt when he opened the door.

"Oh my god, I threw those out two years ago," Marti said, as Hank launched himself at Oliver's chest. Fleeter of foot than Marti, Oliver managed to step back in time to avoid the brunt of the impact. Hank dropped on all fours and pranced around Oliver's feet, licking the bare patch of skin above his knee.

Oliver knelt on the exposed knee and put his arms around Hank's neck. Holding him in one place was usually an effective way to calm the dog down. Finally he looked up at Marti and asked, "Threw what out?"

"Those sweats. They were in the bottom of the bag for the thrift shop. In the trunk of the car and—"

"Under a blanket. It was like you were trying to smuggle out a celebrity."

"So you pulled them out and hid them for a year?"

"Closer to two."

"And carried them across the country in that backpack? And back?"

He shrugged. "I like them. I keep stuff I like."

Marti tried not to read too much into that. "Well, you're better at hiding things than I am, obviously."

"Don't know about that." He grabbed Hank's muzzle and turned it to the light. "What happened here?"

It took her a couple of seconds to remember the racoon incident of three nights before. So much had happened since then. She gave Oliver the broad brushstrokes. When she got to the part about Mrs. Galloway and the dead cat, Oliver got to his feet and leaned on the doorframe. Hank wandered around the room, and then climbed up on the bed. He rolled over on his side with a contented sigh.

"Wait a second," Oliver said, as she rushed on to describe the next escape the following night. "Let's go back to this dead cat."

"It's all I got," Marti said. She was shivering now, from nerves and relief to be sharing all of this with the only person who really cared. "Anyway, I managed to lure Hank home from the drugstore. But look what arrived in my inbox the next day." She pulled off her mittens, cued up the video and handed the phone to Oliver.

He watched it once, twice, three times, increasing the magnification each time and holding it a little closer to his face. "Huh," he said at last. "I always liked that bra."

It had been a birthday gift years ago. Marti had complained that it was impractical, and really more of a gift for him. So Oliver had agreed to get another gift just for her. The next day he'd presented her with a ring. *The* ring. She twisted it absent-mindedly now, wondering again, if he'd really had it for weeks, like he'd said. Or if she'd guilt-tripped him into proposing when he wasn't ready.

"Yes," he said now, with his signature twisted smile. "I really did have it for weeks. We've already established that I know how to hide things."

"I didn't... Well, I..." She put her mittens back on. "I liked that bra, too." She hadn't worn it for years, but after Oliver had come back to Dorset Hills, she'd pulled it out. It was a bit small, but instead of feeling constricting, it felt like a hug. "Past tense. After Hank dragged it around town, there wasn't much left of it."

"It'll live on in memory." Waggling the phone at her, he asked, "So what's up with this?"

"I don't know."

He watched the video one more time. "No one would know it's you except me, probably."

"And the person who took it. I think someone's following me."

"You? Why?"

She pointed past him at Hank, who was now chewing on something. Oliver crossed to the bed and pried his computer mouse out of Hank's jaws. He wiped off the slobber with his T-shirt and inspected it. Then he took the laptop off the bed and moved it to the dresser.

Finally, he turned back to Marti and seemed to register that she was freezing. "You can come in, Marti. I won't bite."

She did, closing the door behind her and leaning on it. Her legs felt wobbly and she was still breathing in short, panicky gasps. "I'm scared."

"Don't let your imagination run away with you. It's probably just a joke."

"I don't think so. I think someone wants me out of my job."

"Already? You just started."

"It's not making me any friends. There's a trainer who runs with the Rescue Mafia, and Cliff Whorley hates me."

"Whorley. That guy's an ass." Oliver moved around straightening the room and piling things on the dresser out of Hank's reach. "You could always ask for a transfer."

That she couldn't. It would be tantamount to admitting failure, and failure wasn't in her professional lexicon. Every employer, starting with her first summer job, had given her outstanding performance reviews. This job may not be a good fit, but a creep with a camera couldn't drive her out. She'd leave on her terms.

"Oliver, you need to keep Hank. Whoever is targeting me has found my Achilles heel. I'm judging other people's dogs while my own is a troublemaker."

Hank was lolling on his back on the bed now, with a sock in his mouth. He glanced at them coyly, to make sure it was noticed. Shaking his head, Oliver reached for Hank's leash and pulled him off the bed. He took the sock from the dog's mouth and threw it onto the dresser as well.

"Dorset Hills is a joke," he said.

"It is right now. And I doubt I will last long in this job, but I don't want to be chased out of it. I've worked too hard to be humiliated like that, don't you think?"

Oliver ran his fingers through his silver hair. He was softening. "But my workshops are long here. Hank would be on his own a lot."

"I've got a great walker who will come this far. The rest of the time you lock him in the bathroom with a chew stick. I brought his stuff."

He glared at her. "You were that sure I'd relent?"

"Just hopeful," she said, smiling.

Hank's leash was still in Oliver's hand, and the dog sniffed the mottled brown carpet, drawing in the history of the resort. Moving in a circle, Hank wrapped his leash around Marti's legs and continued, drawing her closer to Oliver in a tightening loop. She had forgotten how good Oliver smelled. It was a combination of the cedar and coriander soap he always used and the magic of his own genes. She desperately wanted to lay her head on his shoulder, but was afraid he would back away, or worse, push her away. So she stood within inches of his chest, staring at his old, ratty T-shirt, and waited for him to make a move.

When he finally did, it was only to set his free hand on her shoulder gently. "Marti, this will all die down. You know how Dog Town blows everything out of proportion. And then people finally get fixated on something new."

"I know, I know. In the meantime, Hank will be better with you."

He sighed, and she could hear in its depth that this was costing him something—something more than inconvenience. She knew she should ask—should bring up the invisible barrier that was keeping them just inches apart and straining slightly backward against the leash Hank had bound them with, but it was so hard. How could it be so hard to talk to her own husband, when they'd shared their lives and a bed for so many years?

That was ridiculous too, she decided. She would break this old habit of silence, starting today. "Oliver, I'm sorry."

"It's okay, Marti. I can work around Hank."

She felt his breath on her forehead and leaned in. Oliver didn't move away. "It's not just Hank," she said. "I'm sorry for—"

A loud knock silenced her.

Hank leapt toward the door, and as he had them ensnared, the move knocked them off balance. Oliver tried to brace himself on something, and failing, spun his arms and clipped Marti in the ear. She fell backwards, pulling Oliver over on top of her. Dropping the leash, he got his arms out in time to keep his full weight off her. He swore first, she echoed the curse, and then they both burst out laughing. Hank let out a growling woof at the door, but they ignored him, staring at each other. The heat was rising inside Marti's parka; she hadn't felt that warm for months. Staring into Oliver's eyes, she hoped whoever had knocked at the door would go away and let them continue their conversation horizontally.

The knock came again, more insistently. A woman's voice called, "Oliver?"

Oliver pushed up and off Marti so fast that she felt a gust of cool air flushing away all the reconciliation pheromones.

Grabbing Hank's leash, Oliver pulled him back from the door and opened it. "Deanna. Hi."

Deanna was deceptively girl-next-door, with her shiny dark hair in a casual ponytail. From her spot on the floor, Marti could see that Deanna's yoga gear was perfectly matched under a jacket left casually open. Her make-up was subtle, and she left all the talking to the big diamond studs in her ears.

Craning around Oliver, Deanna saw Marti on the floor, while Hank strained against his leash, trying to reach the guest. "Oh, I'm sorry," she said. "I'm interrupting."

"No, it's fine," Oliver said. "Deanna, this is my dog, Hank, and —" he half-turned. "Marti. She brought Hank to visit."

Marti's heart gave a fragile flutter in her chest. Hank was "his dog." She was just Marti. Not "my wife, Marti." Not even, "my ex, Marti." Just Marti, some woman who landed on the floor of my hotel room. A dogsitter, perhaps.

Deanna pushed past Oliver and held out her hand to shake Marti's. "I'm Deanna, Oliver's writing coach. We're collaborating on a screenplay."

"That's great," Marti said, releasing Deanna's hand.

With Hank's leash in his right hand, Oliver offered his left to pull Marti up. That's when she noticed he wasn't wearing his wedding ring.

Marti scrambled to her feet. "Well, I'd better be going." She edged around Deanna and out the open door. "I'll let you guys get to work."

Deanna stood in the open doorway, looking after her. "Hey, didn't you forget something?"

Marti kept going. If she turned, she would probably cry.

"Like, the dog?" Deanna called. "There are no dogs allowed in the lodge."

Now Marti stopped and turned. "I guess you aren't from around here, Deanna. Dogs rule this county."

Deanna turned to Oliver and put her hand on his chest, saying something Marti couldn't hear. Meanwhile, Hank manoeuvred into a position that could only mean one thing. "Hank," she called. "Down! Off!"

Hank rose onto his hind legs, clamped Deanna around her waist, and started humping. If she hadn't had years of yoga practice under her Lycra, Deanna probably would have toppled. Instead, she twisted and lifted one knee against Hank's chest. "Get off me, you," she said. But when Hank clamped on, he meant business. So Deanna got him with her knee again and gave him such a shove that the dog actually yelped and fell over on his side.

"Hey," Marti said. "Stop that!"

"Well, he—" Deanna began.

"I could have you charged with animal abuse," Marti said, storming back up the path to the cabin. "Heaven help you if you ended up in my court."

"Marti," Oliver said. "Take it easy."

"Take it easy? You let her hurt Hank."

Deanna moved out of the way before Marti got to the door. Leaning down, Marti grabbed Hank's leash and gave it a sharp tug. "Let's go."

"Wait," Oliver called after them. "I can—"

His words were drowned out by the blood pounding in Marti's ears. "Never mind," she called back. "I'll take care of Hank. I shouldn't have come."

CHAPTER 14

*K*inney Butterfield proved herself invaluable before she'd even hit the streets of Dorset Hills as a dog cop. Marti had called Kinney in before the ink dried on her contract, and asked her to pull together an open house event at the CCD. And Kinney did—in one day. She got the word out on social media using irresistible incentives: "dogs welcome" and "free coffee." Going above and beyond, she decorated the office with beautiful dog portraits on loan from local artists. It transformed the place from forbidding to fun.

On Sunday afternoon, people started pouring into the office and courthouse. Most came out of curiosity, and stayed on for the company.

Marti worked her way through the crowed, pressing hands and patting furry heads. Kinney was the official showrunner, keeping coffee cups full, and making introductions. Unofficially, she shadowed Cori Hogan, who was wandering around like she owned the place. The room was warm, but Cori had her bird-flipping gloves on anyway.

"Genius idea, my friend," Tonna said, following Marti into her office and closing the door. "What did the mayor say?"

"His exact words were 'good luck,'" Marti told her. "He's a big fan of community-building, or so he says. He sent one of his advisors, and if the vibe is right, later, he'll stop by."

"I can't wait to meet him," Tonna said. "Now that I know he's been snooping around my business. I feel pretty special."

Marti shushed her. "Keep it down, Tons. I'm barely staying a step ahead of trouble as it is."

"Anything more on the vid?" Tonna whispered.

"It hasn't been posted anywhere else as far as I can tell. Only you and Oliver know about it. And of course, DogFraudBuster."

"Such intrigue. But I think it's perfectly clear who's behind it. Only one person wants you out of this fancy office."

They both turned to see Cliff staring in at them. He nodded, before heading off to tail Kinney, who was tailing Cori.

"I want to do some good here if I can," Marti said. "Even if I have to ruffle a few feathers before I go."

"I like this new Marti," Tonna said, grinning. "I think Oliver will, too."

But her grin faded as Marti filled her in on their visit the day before. "He seemed to know this Deanna pretty well, considering they supposedly only met this week," she said. "Maybe that's the real reason he wanted to dump Hank."

"Jury's still out," Tonna said. "I've seen the way Oliver watches you, and that feeling doesn't change overnight."

"Ladies!" The door cracked open and Cori Hogan stepped in. "Can I join the party?"

Marti gave Cori her best political smile. "Cori, you *are* the party. You're the only guest on the agenda today."

Cori had agreed to give a short talk about dog leadership to interested participants.

"What do you want me to cover?" she asked.

"Play it by ear," Marti said. "Just maybe try not to alienate everyone."

Tonna laughed. "There's no better trainer in Dorset Hills than Cori."

"As if you'd know," Cori said. "You won't let me get my hands on that little Diva."

"Sssssh," Tonna said. "Place could be bugged."

There was a gentle knock on the door, and a woman with smooth dark hair and a wide smile waved. Under her other arm was a shaggy red dog that looked like a teddy bear.

"George," they all said at once. His photo had been in the news after the dognapping, and everyone in town knew him.

Marti knew Mim Gardiner quite well from the health consultations in her previous job, and introduced her to Tonna. Cori greeted Mim with a familiar smile and a quick flash of neon orange. Was there anyone in town she didn't know?

"So good to see you, Mim," Marti said. "You look well."

"I am," Mim said. "This is our first official outing since the… event."

"I'm so sorry about what happened," Marti said. "George looks happy."

"Scrappier than ever," she said. "I thought I'd join Cori's class and see if we can't learn something."

"I'll turn this spoiled brat around in no time," Cori said. She held out her fingers for George to sniff and he shoved his head under her hand for a rub.

"All dogs love Cori, it seems," Marti said.

"Especially the bad ones," Cori said. "You know why? They all want to be good. Which means they need good leaders."

Kinney poked her head in to collect Cori, and Tonna went with them. Mim lingered to say, "I just wanted to apologize, Marti. I have the feeling this isn't where you wanted to be. You were a dream come true to the community health sector. It somehow seems like this whole dog court thing is a reaction to what happened with George."

Mim held out her free hand and Marti took it. "No, no, don't worry," she told Mim. "This is a great opportunity."

"Then why do you look like you've aged five years in the past week?" Mim asked. "I'm speaking as a nurse, now."

Marti blinked a few times. Her tear ducts seemed loaded and ready to fire these days. "I haven't been sleeping well, that's all. It's an adjustment."

Mim went in for a hug and Marti didn't resist. She couldn't beat the huggers, it seemed, so she might as well join them. George squirmed between them and then licked Marti's face.

Camera flashes made them part. Leslie Longland was directing a photographer to get pictures of Mim and Marti.

"There you go, back on the front page," Marti said, leading Mim out of the office. She shielded her from Leslie and escorted her into the courtroom, where the chairs had been folded and moved to allow a dozen owners and dogs to congregate.

Cori was sitting in Marti's chair on the dais, spinning gently. "The air is thin up here in your ivory tower, Marti, but oh, what a view."

"Off," Marti said. "Or should that be 'down'?"

Everyone laughed except Cliff, who was standing at the side of the room with the mayor's advisor. "That is highly—"

"Audacious," Marti interrupted. "Cori is known for her razor-sharp wit, as well as her way with dogs. We're lucky she's agreed to talk us through some of the challenges facing dog owners today."

"Female dog owners in particular," Cori said, jumping lightly from her perch. "I notice there are no male dog owners in the room, and more than 80 per cent of my clients are women. Isn't that interesting?"

"Why is that?" Tonna asked. "Men have bad dogs, too."

"There are no bad dogs, despite what you might hear to the contrary," Cori said. "But yes, men certainly have training issues. I find in my practice, however, that men are slower to come forward to admit they have a problem. That said, I believe more women struggle with being the boss. And I'm going to tell you why over the next few sessions. Today, we're just going to socialize a bit. Let the dogs get comfortable."

Marti sat on the edge of the dais and watched Mim and others walk up to each other and chat, as their dogs sniffed and pawed and tried to play. A pretty woman with a sweet little beagle had slipped in late, and several of the others hurried towards her. Remi and Leo, it sounded like. Marti definitely felt like the odd one out—here on her own turf.

Cori circled the room, meeting each person, and settling an excited dog here and there. Despite having so many dogs in close confines there wasn't a whiff of trouble.

About 20 minutes later, however, a hush fell over the room. In the doorway stood a strikingly beautiful blond woman with a large, red, nicely groomed dog at her side. It was like a switch flipped in the room. Suddenly half the dogs were barking and rearing. George wasn't one of them. His tail wagged furiously as the woman walked over to Mim. The red dog greeted George with composure.

Mim beckoned Marti over and introduced her to her best friend, Arianna Torrance, who also happened to be George's breeder.

"Lovely to meet you. Call me Ari," she said. "And this my side-kick, Hugo, who also happens to be George's sire"

Hugo sniffed Marti's hand and his fringed tail fanned gently.

"He likes you," Ari said. "Hugo's discriminating. With such high ratings, I feel like the CCD will be in good hands."

Cori came over and nodded at Ari. "Honestly, Ari, you know better than to bring Hugo to an event like this."

"What? He's the perfect gentleman," Ari said. Hugo sat by her side and kept his eyes on his mistress.

"It's not about him. Look at the rest of the buffoons." They looked around and it was as if laughing gas for dogs had been piped into the room. They all got silly.

"Right, Hugo's got his parts," Tonna said. "That's why I only allow neutered dogs at my club. Boys and their hormones."

"You were saying?" Mayor Bradshaw used his deepest car-commercial voice, causing all the women in earshot to titter.

Mim whispered something in Ari's ear, and she quietly excused herself with Hugo. All the dogs settled again, as if by magic.

The mayor was quickly surrounded by women and dogs. The reporter stayed close by and the photographer snapped off shot after shot. Looking over the crowd, the mayor gave Marti a wink. It was subtle, but not subtle enough for Cliff to miss. He gathered his guy squad and left the courtroom.

The mayor, on the other hand, stayed far longer than expected, chatting at length with Tonna, and Ari, when she came back in without Hugo. Mim he avoided like the plague.

Finally, Kinney Butterfield tapped her watch to suggest winding things down.

Marti thanked the mayor for coming, and when the applause subsided, she singled Cori out too. "We're so grateful she agreed to share her expertise with all of us," she said.

"How much do the classes cost?" Tonna asked, just to give Marti an opening.

"The CCD is picking up the tab," Marti said. "We're committed to creating happy owners and obedient dogs. Check our website for details."

Cori raised a gloved hand. "I'm always happy to devote my time and services to a good cause. But just to be clear, I don't work for the CCD, or anyone else." She waved at Leslie Longland, who was taking notes. "Did you catch that?"

Marti turned quickly to the mayor, but he'd vanished.

CHAPTER 15

"*I* object!"

Marti gave her leg a savage pinch through her robes to try to keep herself awake. Even a lively hearing and a cold breeze couldn't keep her alert, let alone agreeable. She was running on so little sleep and so much worry that her patience was thinning. "You can't object, Mr. Lobo. This isn't a formal courtroom."

"It sure looks like a courtroom," he said, with a sweeping gesture.

"The folding chairs are a giveaway," Cori Hogan said. "We're all part of the play and don't know it. Surreal."

"Thanks for the commentary, Ms. Hogan," Marti said. "Let's continue with Act One, then, shall we?"

Mr. Lobo persisted. "How do I register my complaint that she's full of—"

"Consider it registered. And I tend to agree with you."

"Excuse me," Cori said. "I have evidence to prove neutering can prevent a dog from reaching his full size and development. In some circles, it's now considered inhumane." Cori rustled a sheaf of papers. "Allow me to read…"

"No thank you, Ms. Hogan. I don't need to hear the latest thinking on neutering to know that Ms. Beal's dog should not be relentlessly mounting Mr. Lobo's dog in the street." She filled the gap before Cori could. "Or anywhere else. Mr. Lobo has a right to walk his dog unmolested in his own neighborhood."

The defendant was an impressive-looking Bouvier, who strained at his harness to get to the complainant, Lacy, a delicate Italian greyhound with a perpetual quiver.

"See, the word 'unmolested' suggests that you're projecting human emotions onto the dogs, Judge," Cori said. "In the dog world, mounting is more typically a sign of dominance than sexuality. I believe that my client, Moose, is merely communicating in canine language, that he is the top dog on the block. In the wild, wolves thrive in a hierarchical pack structure."

"Dorset Hills hardly qualifies as the wild, Ms. Hogan. I believe we can have different expectations of our modern day wolves here." Cori started to speak again, and Marti raised her voice. "I understand your 'dogs will be dogs' argument, but our expectations are really for their owners."

Marti had to give Cori credit. Since she'd extracted some lenience from Marti earlier in the week, she'd seemingly become a community advocate for every dog facing his day in court. No wonder she'd been so anxious to be seen as arms-length from the CCD.

"Judge, be reasonable," Cori said. "It's just humping. Dogs hump."

"I object," Mr. Lobo said again. "This isn't just humping. Moose is all over Lacy all the time. He humps her from every angle. He knocked her right over last week and kept humping air. I don't think he even noticed she was down. I want the City to order that dog neutered."

"He is neutered," Moose's owner said. "He had the latest laser procedure. It's like a vasectomy."

"It's much healthier for the dog," Cori said. "Male dogs that are snipped too early often end up with longer legs in proportion to their body, not to mention a higher incidence of cancer. I want the City to recognize that alternate strategies for neutering are valid."

"That's beyond my purview, Ms. Hogan," Marti said. "And this isn't the platform for your crusades. I'm here to decide whether Moose's behavior is impinging on his neighbors' capacity to go about their lives in peace. And by 'neighbors,' I mean the ones who pay taxes. In addition to Mr. Lobo, I have complaints on file from three other dog owners about Moose's proclivities."

"He's sterile," Moose's owner said.

Mr. Lobo glared at her. "I don't care if he's shooting blanks. Lacy is spayed anyway. I just want to be able to walk her down the street without this big oaf knocking her over. Judge, this dog needs to lose his package."

Marti pressed her lips together. She couldn't afford to lose it, no matter how tired and giddy she felt.

"In Dorset Hills, people still have choices about their dog's health care," Cori said. "The municipality can't order a dog to be castrated."

"In fact, there is provision for the court to make such decisions, Ms. Hogan," Marti said.

"Where?" Cori demanded. "Please point that out to me in the regulations."

"I don't need to point anything out to you, Ms. Hogan. You are not the owner of the accused."

"I'm representing the accused. His owner wants to know where the regulations stipulate that you have the right to enforce castration. Right?" She turned to Moose's owner and Ms. Beal nodded.

Marti closed her eyes and took a deep breath. Cori was determined to turn every hearing into a circus, no doubt to embarrass the City. She was good at it, too. The only reason there hadn't been more media coverage was that the mayor was exerting influence. That wouldn't work forever. "Stand down, Ms. Hogan. I've made my decision. Moose's owners have a choice: they can keep him well away from other dogs at all times. Or they can have him neutered in the old-fashioned way, and work on his obedience."

Moose's owner and Cori spoke over each other, both bleating "unfair."

"Judge, Moose is only ten months old," Cori said. "Keeping him away from other dogs would negatively affect his socialization."

"That's why I've offered neutering as an option," Marti said. "It may not stop the behavior, as you know. Many dogs continue to mount after neutering."

"My point exactly," Cori said. "It's a dominance display. So it's unfair to order the dog neutered when it may not have the desired impact."

"Moose's owners have a choice here," Marti said. "They can have Moose neutered and see how it goes. If the dog continues to make life unpleasant for his neighbors—and they complain to the City—we'll be back here again. But neutering improves his odds of being able to mix with other dogs." She glanced over at Moose, who had certainly grown into his name. "It appears to my unschooled eye that Moose is everything a mature Bouvier should be."

"But Judge, you are sentencing this dog to a life of isolation," Cori said. "He'll become socially stunted and frustrated."

"We all have to make difficult choices in life, Ms. Hogan." Seeing half a dozen mouths open to complain, Marti raised her gavel and brought it down. "And we're adjourned."

THE MAIL WAS SITTING in a neat pile to the left of the door when Marti got home. She picked it up, flipped through it, and unlocked the door.

Hank did his usual dance of joy, and she nudged him aside with her knee as she reached for the light switch. Heaving himself onto his hind legs, he put his paws on her chest and licked her face.

Bits of chewed-up paper were stuck to his muzzle. Looking down, she saw the rug in the hall was covered with shredded paper snow. Marti shoved Hank aside and picked up some of the larger pieces. It looked like a print out of a photo on white paper. Dropping to her hands and knees she tried to assemble the photo like a puzzle. There appeared to be multiple copies, because she kept coming up with repeat pieces, just torn in new shapes.

When she discerned Hank in the photo, she started to grab pieces and assemble faster. Hank paced over the pieces again and again, making the job even tougher.

Finally, she noticed an intact sheet of paper under the hall table. It seemed like the person who'd dropped it in the mail slot kept trying with copy after copy until he'd managed to slip one by the canine shredder inside.

Marti sat back on her heels and stared at the paper. It was a photo of cabin number three at Hilltop Inn, where Oliver was staying. Marti was in the foreground, with her back to the camera.

Hank's beautiful markings were visible in profile even as he gripped Deanna around the waist. Luckily it was a still shot, and she was spared seeing Hank humping her husband's new girl-friend in perpetuity.

Marti's eye drifted down the page to a single word at the bottom in an understated 12-point font:

"Fraud."

CHAPTER 16

*M*arti drove slowly along her street with her head out the window and her phone to her ear.

"Can you repeat that?" Tonna asked. "You're tailing someone, or being tailed?"

"Both," Marti said. It was no wonder Tonna was confused. The words had come out in a torrent, and the wind was blowing in Marti's face as she tried to make out Hank's paw prints in the snow. Even with the streetlights on, it was dark. Dorset Hills-in-winter dark, which seemed darker than anywhere else. "Hank got out of the back yard and I'm following him now. Can you come and help?"

She heard a slam at the other end of the phone. "On my way. Keep talking."

"Put the phone on hands-free," Marti said. "The driving is terrible."

"You've got the phone hanging out the window," Tonna said. "I can tell."

"I have to. I keep losing Hank's trail. He was swerving like a drunk."

"How'd he escape this time?"

"Through the back gate. I was in the yard too, scooping poop." She thought about telling Tonna what she'd found in that two-day-old frozen poop, but she didn't want to get sidetracked.

"And the gate was open?"

"I double checked it was shut this morning, and the walker uses the front door."

"So you think someone set Hank up?"

"Looks that way. I got home to find at least five copies of a print-out stuck through my mail slot. It was a photo of Hank humping Oliver's new girlfriend at the hotel. He chewed through every version of Oliver's face but missed the word 'fraud' five times."

"So you were looking for Oliver's face?" Tonna's grin was audible.

Marti almost drove onto the sidewalk, craning out the window for Hank's prints, until she found them again. "What?"

"You heard me. What about this Deanna's face?"

"Five good copies," Marti said. "I like to think the flavor was bitter."

Tonna laughed. "You haven't entirely lost your sense of humor."

"The humor gauge is hovering perilously close to the red zone."

A van pulled up behind Marti and flashed its warning lights. "It's me," Tonna said. As if Marti could miss an orange van. Tonna had gotten a deal on it because of the color, and it served as a dog bus half the time anyway. "Pull over."

Marti turned the corner so that they could park on a quieter side street, and continue the search on foot. Giving Tonna a hug, Marti led the way forward again. She was alarmed at how many intersections Hank had crossed on his mission. "I don't see how he got so far, so fast," she said.

Kneeling, Tonna poked around in the snow. "It's like he's after something. You can see he keeps stopping and starting again. Like following a trail of breadcrumbs."

"If there were any, he ate the evidence," Marti said. "I figured he's just looking for Oliver."

"Right, so let's get back to Oliver," Tonna said.

"Must we?"

"Yeah, we must. Someone who doesn't like dogs is trying to steal your husband."

Pointing at the tracks that turned right onto the next street, Marti said, "If she's able to get to Oliver that easily, he wants to be stolen."

"So that's it? You're just giving up?"

"What am I supposed to do?"

Tonna leaned down, scooped a pile of slushy snow and hurled it at Marti's head from close range. It hit her temple and trickled down one cheek.

"Wow, you're not even going to complain about getting hit in the head with a snowball. You really have given up on yourself," Tonna said.

Marti wiped the snow away with one mitten. "That's a little harsh."

"I'm trying to get you to fight for what you want. If what you want is Oliver."

Marti trudged on in silence, with her eyes on the ground.

"Okay, let me restate that," Tonna said. "What you really *should* want is Oliver."

"He walked out on me."

Tonna leaned over to gather another handful of snow. Marti caught her arm. "Don't you dare."

"That's a start," Tonna said, grinning.

"Let me restate this: Oliver walked out on me."

"Marti, that might be true as far as the final door slam goes. But from what I could see, you had one foot out the door emotionally when I met you."

"You're crazy," Marti said. "That was four years ago."

"I bet even longer. Maybe you never had both feet in."

Marti turned to stare at her. "What are you saying?"

"I'm speaking truth to power, Judge. You figure it out." Tonna's grin faded as she peered over Marti's shoulder. "Hank," she said. And then, "Oh no."

Marti spun, her heart in her throat, but Hank was simply sniffing around in the parking lot outside the CCD courthouse. When he saw them, he came running over, tail wagging. But when Marti reached out to grab his leash, he dodged her and went back to his sniffing.

Tonna was staring ahead, with her mouth hanging open.

"Hank's okay, Tonna. What's wrong?"

Pointing at the new CCD sign over the door, Tonna said, "That's what's wrong."

Lettering in thick yellow paint covered the sign. It read: "FRAUD."

Tonna squeezed Marti's arm and said, "We should call the cops."

"No. I don't want to draw attention to this."

"It's going to escalate, Marti. First the video, then the flyer, now this. What next?"

"Someone wants me out of office, that's all."

"Well, they're taking the campaign pretty seriously. I really think you need to tell someone. If not the police, then the mayor."

Marti shook her head. "If the mayor finds out, I'll lose my job."

"You hate your job."

"I don't hate it." Marti stared around at the empty parking lot, looking for clues. The City hadn't installed the new lighting she'd requested yet. Even so, she could see tracks from several cars, including her own.

"Here's what you said a few nights ago: 'I hate my job.' Has it improved this week?"

"I said I hate dog court, which is still true. I think the No Bad

Dogs regime is taking Dorset Hills down a bad path that will bite this city in the butt. But I enjoyed the open house, for example. And hiring Kinney. I feel like there's potential for the CCD itself to do some good here. Then I can extricate myself gracefully, when the time is right."

Tonna pulled a bag of dog treats out of her pocket and called Hank. He was still nosing around in the slush and didn't even look up. "That's weird. Hank loves these treats." Crinkling the bag, she walked toward him. He didn't come, but he didn't move away, and Tonna was able to grab his collar.

Marti came over and hooked up his leash. "Do you think the hardware store is still open?"

～

"YOU LOOK RIDICULOUS," Tonna said, as Marti pulled the goggles over her mask.

Marti mumbled something and Tonna cupped her ear. Pulling down the mask, Marti said, "Can you quit speaking truth to power? I've had a full dose for one night."

"The guy at the hardware store said this solvent is non-toxic."

"Well, I'm not taking any chances," Marti said. "My luck hasn't been great lately."

"Let me." Tonna tried to take the spray bottle from Marti's rubber-gloved hand.

Marti shook her head and climbed the ladder. She sprayed the capital F first, and watched in relief as the paint started to break up and drip onto the snow below. "Sponge it, Marti. Now, it looks like pee."

Marti wiped up the drizzle and continued. Within twenty minutes, the sign was wiped clean. Tonna's flashlight revealed only the faintest hint of lettering, and Marti was satisfied no one would notice anything amiss.

Tonna shone the light on Marti's Jeep, where Hank was sitting behind the wheel, with his tongue hanging out. "That dog is something else."

"Try speaking truth to that power," Marti said, loading the ladder into Tonna's van. "Your place?"

"You got it."

~

POURING wine into Marti's glass, Tonna said, "Hang in there, my friend. This too shall pass."

"I feel like I have a big yellow F on my forehead," Marti said. "Because I really am a fraud and a hypocrite. Today I argued for castration when my own dog is an unneutered humper."

"And Cori argued that castration doesn't make a difference when only Sunday she said Ari's breeding sire was affecting the other dogs just by being in the room. In other words, she's a fraud and a hypocrite, too. That's how it goes in politics, my friend."

Marti led the way into the family room. "I'm no politician."

"Could have fooled me."

Grabbing a pillow, Marti tossed it at her friend. "Stop kicking me when I'm down."

"Then get up. Accept your role in this farce and play it well. In a year, dog court will be a distant memory in Dorset Hills."

They sank into their usual seats and stretched cold feet toward the fireplace. Hank flaked out between them, tired from his adventure.

"Seriously, it's all I can do to keep a straight face in court. The whole thing is ludicrous."

"It's going to be a social media sensation. Right now, in the surrounding towns, graphic artists are preparing their satires."

"And I'll have the starring role."

"You'll be linked to this forever with millions of hits. That's why I think you should get out while you can."

Marti groaned. "Maybe you're right. But how?"

"Like I said, you have skills in the political arena. Strategize your way out."

"I don't even know where to start. I can think of more people who want me out than want me in. Cliff. Cori. Even Leslie Longland, probably." Marti stared at the fire. "I should just get myself fired."

"That's one option. It's working with Oliver."

Marti hurled another cushion at her but she blocked it easily. "We covered that earlier. Moving on."

"Just pointing out a recurring theme in your life. Some people pay big bucks for observations like mine."

"By choice."

"Choice is the key word, my friend. I don't understand why you're just letting choices be made for you, when you could make them yourself."

Marti considered hurling the last cushion, but she was too comfortable. "What about you? Do you always make good choices?"

"Mostly."

"Please. You had a chance to franchise your business last year and turned it down, against expert advice."

"That was a reasoned decision. I didn't want to sink my teeth too far into Dog Town. In case I want to move on."

"Okay, so it's better to make a poor decision than no decision at all."

"I would say yes to that."

"Then I'd argue with your logic, Tonna. And one of us is a judge."

Tonna was still grinning, but she sat up straight. "I'm happy with my decision. I wanted to keep my business small and personal."

"I see your point, but in the past six months, two upstarts have copied your model and stolen twenty per cent of your business."

"Probably more, but I'm getting by."

"You originated the exclusive dog club in Dog Town. Everyone else is just riding on your coattails."

"There's enough business for all," Tonna said.

"How Zen of you. I think this is really about your fear of settling down. You're happy with your business, but don't want to fully commit. You're happy with Levi, but don't want to commit."

"Sounds like we have something in common."

"I married Oliver. I'm committed." Marti held up her left hand, and her rings sparkled in the firelight. "And by the way, I found Oliver's wedding ring."

"What? Where?"

"In Hank's poop. He must have found it in the hotel room and swallowed it."

"Yes!" Tonna clapped. "We have our answer to the missing ring."

"I guess he took it off to improve his screenwriting speed."

"Whatever. You don't know why." Closing her eyes for a second, Tonna said, "I hate to ask, but I gotta."

Marti laughed. "You bet I plucked that ring out of the poop. It's in detox as we speak."

"You're going to put that ring back on Oliver's finger," Tonna said. "None the worse for its journey."

CHAPTER 17

*M*arti liked to be first to arrive in the courtroom. It gave her a chance to size everyone up as they filed into the room. Although she was no expert on dog behavior, she could often get a good read on the accused by his or her entrance.

Angus McFadden's arrival suggested he was an ass. A stocky Scottish terrier, he trotted ahead of his owner, straining at the leash and bristling with attitude. He paused at the foot of the dais and stared up at Marti. One stubby back leg started to rise.

"Angus," hissed his owner, Jenny Kent. "Don't even think about it." Looking up at Marti, she added, "Sorry, Judge."

Marti just smiled. She liked Jenny, although her popular hair salon was a gossip hub. Marti had avoided it, like most of her usual haunts, after Oliver left in November, so her flyaway winter hair was in dire need of highlights. Maybe Jenny would talk about how she was letting herself go, and say no wonder Oliver left. Deanna had spectacular hair.

But today Marti was the judge. Angus and Jenny were here to defend themselves against complaints from the Dorset Hills Elementary School, represented by Principal Felicity Chan.

As everyone settled into their seats, Marti looked around for

Cori and heaved a sigh of relief. She had a bit of a hangover and was not up to sparring today.

"Good morning, everyone," she said. "Let's get started. I've read the complaint. Mrs. Kent's daughter, Poppy, took a pet home from her first-grade classroom over Christmas, and he didn't make it back."

"Hannibal," Principal Chan said. "A white rat that had been with the school for three years."

"Mrs. Kent," Marti said. "Would you like to tell us what happened to Hannibal?"

Jenny stood. "Judge, we had warned Poppy to leave Hannibal in her bedroom at all times. Unfortunately, we weren't clear that Angus needed to be banned from the bedroom."

"So Angus came into the bedroom, and…"

"Poppy was sitting on a chair with Hannibal in her lap…"

Jenny's voice faltered and Marti nudged her gently. "And then…"

"Angus… Well, Angus grabbed Hannibal. Gave him one shake and that was it."

There was a collective gasp from the school side of the room. "That's horrible," Principal Chan said.

"Look, I could have lied," Jenny said. "I could have said Hannibal had escaped or something. But Poppy was absolutely traumatized. I felt we needed to deal with this in an upfront fashion. So I called the teacher first thing on Monday and offered to replace Hannibal."

"You don't replace a pet that easily," Principal Chan said. "The entire class was devastated."

There was a quiet click as the door of the courtroom closed. Cori was making her way to sit in the empty seat beside Jenny. "Sorry I'm late, Judge," she said.

"Seems like you're everywhere these days, Ms. Hogan," Marti said.

"Just trying to help out where I can." Cori flipped her the glove.

"As I was saying," Principal Chan continued, "the children were devastated. We held a funeral for Hannibal."

"For which I sent three dozen cupcakes," Jenny said.

"Decorated with whiskers and beads for eyes," Principal Chan said. "It was in extremely poor taste."

"All of them were eaten," Jenny retorted. "How devastated could the class have been? Certainly not as upset as Poppy, who had to witness the event."

"It's unfortunate for Poppy that her parents keep a dangerous dog. This time Hannibal, next time… who knows?" Principal Chan raised her eyebrows significantly at Marti. "It could be far worse."

"Are you suggesting Angus would hurt a person?" Jenny bristled, and Angus jumped to his feet at the sound of his name.

"Allow me," Cori said, pulling Jenny down, and then standing herself. "Judge, I'd like to speak on behalf of the accused."

"Of course you would," Marti said, rubbing her eyes.

"Someone has to speak up for the dogs in this town," Cori said.

"Well, the dogs are lucky to have you, Ms. Hogan."

Cori stared at Marti and Marti stared back. Finally, Principal Chan cleared her throat to move things along.

"Right, so what I wanted to say is that Scottish terriers are bred to kill rodents," Cori said. "Angus was following his instincts. While it was unfortunate for both Poppy and her classmates—"

"How about Hannibal?" Principal Chan asked.

"And of course, Hannibal," Cori continued, "this was clearly not an act of aggression that is likely to be repeated unless another rodent comes home."

"Poppy told me her sleeve was ripped in the attack," Principal Chan said. "It could so easily have been her wrist that was punctured. If it weren't for this court, I'd have called Child Protective Services."

"Excuse me?" Jenny jumped up again. "You're saying I'm an unfit parent because my dog killed a rat? How dare you!"

"I'm saying that we can't allow dog aggression to escalate to violence against children. I would not want any child to be put in this situation."

Cori pushed on Jenny's shoulder. "Down."

"Yes, be seated everyone," Marti said. "Remain calm, or I'll call a recess."

"I'm perfectly calm, Judge," Principal Chan said. "I'm just grateful we now have laws in place to prevent this kind of aggression."

"Principal Chan, with all due respect," Cori said, "what is Dorset Hills coming to if dogs can't be dogs? This town got on the map by being the most dog-friendly place in North America. And now the courts are intruding on private family business to—"

"Ms. Hogan, no grandstanding, please," Marti said.

"My point is that the Kents acknowledge they failed to put the necessary safeguards in place for Hannibal. We take our dogs' civility for granted in Dorset Hills, but they are just animals acting on instinct, after all. The Kents had no ill will toward Hannibal or they wouldn't have invited him home for the weekend. They're willing to buy a rat and a new cage for every classroom in the school."

"People can't buy their way out of every crime, Judge," Principal Chan said. "It's important to take accountability and demonstrate it to our children. I believe the regulations would suggest that Angus be banned from Dorset Hills before he causes future harm."

Marti held up her hand. "Jenny. I mean, Mrs. Kent. Has Angus ever aggressed against other animals or people?

"Never, Judge. You know we've talked about him countless times."

"I'm here as a character reference, your honor," Cori said. "I've been training Angus since he was a pup, and he is a perfect example of his breed."

"A killer of rodents?" Marti said.

Cori ignored this. "He is independent and stubborn, no question. But he has never displayed aggression in training classes toward other dogs or children. We also have a letter from his veterinarian saying he's a typical terrier, no more, no less."

"A typical terror, you mean," Principal Chan muttered. Then louder, "Rats have rights, too."

Once again, Marti had to fight back laughter. The toughest part of her job was keeping a straight face.

"You can't separate a child from her dog," Cori said. "Poppy has accepted what Angus did, and still loves him."

Marti asked for statements from the vet and neighbors about Angus' character. She scanned them as her mind spun like a rat on a wheel. She knew what the mayor would want, but she couldn't do it. "Principal Chan, while this was all most unfortunate, I honestly don't believe that Angus is a threat to people. I'll order that the Kents—"

"Judge, what if I have evidence that Mrs. Kent has lied in court?" the Principal asked.

"If it's relevant, I would have to hear it," Marti said.

"Oh, it's relevant." Principal Chan introduced an older man to the court. "Mr. Gratton frequents the dog park nearest the Kents' house. The regular visitors signed a petition asking that Angus be banned from the park."

"Banned from the dog park? Why?" Marti asked.

"Squirrels, Judge. He killed half a dozen, I'm afraid."

"Two," Jenny said.

"A bloodbath," the Principal said.

"There was no blood, ever," Jenny said. "He's very efficient."

Cori rose again. "Again, while I have great fondness for squirrels, they are rodents. And Angus did what he came into the world to do."

"If she lied about that, what else did she lie about?" Principal Chan asked. She looked like the cat who'd eaten the proverbial canary, whereas Jenny had dissolved into tears.

"Oh, my," Marti said. "I am sorry Jenny didn't feel she could be honest here, but the evidence about the squirrels doesn't change my original view that—"

"Judge." A voice boomed from the back of the room. "May I have a word?"

Mayor Bradshaw was standing beside the bust of Dorset Hills' founder. Calling a recess, Marti rose and met the mayor in her office.

"Marti," he said, taking her hand and holding it. "You look tired."

There was no point in hiding it. "I am, yes. I haven't been sleeping well."

"What's the trouble?" he asked, still holding her hand.

"Excitement. Anxiety."

Marti tried to pull her hand away, but he wouldn't let go. For the first time, she seriously considered if Oliver might be right that Bill Bradshaw's interest wasn't just professional. It seemed unlikely, when he had his choice of many available women, but Oliver had always said Marti was oblivious to interest from other men. That was probably true. As far as she was concerned, there had only ever been one man that mattered.

"Tell me about it," the mayor said.

Marti thought carefully. "Sir, it's partly the new job. I'm still finding my way, as you can imagine."

"Of course, Marti. You know I'm here to coach you."

"Thank you, I appreciate that." She gave her hand another tug and he didn't let go. "There's something else, sir."

"Yes?"

He leaned down to look in her eyes, and Marti met them squarely. "My husband came home, sir. I can't even tell you how much I missed him while he was in Seattle."

The mayor released her hand. "How nice for you."

"I've hardly seen him, since he's at a writing retreat, but just knowing he's nearby makes such a difference."

"Oliver is a lucky man," he said. "And how is your new role here suiting you?"

His eyes were sharp now, as if he were sizing her up. She suspected he'd heard things he didn't like, and there were plenty to choose from. Under the robes and down vest, she broke out in a sweat.

"The hearings are challenging, sir. I won't lie."

"I know you'll make the right choices for Dorset Hills. Our reputation is in your hands."

"Well, sir, I think that's over—"

"Now, now." He was back to interrupting her. "I gave you this job because I know you always do the right thing. You're the consummate public servant, Marti."

"Really, I—"

"No, I won't hear a word of thanks," he said. "We're lucky to have you up on that dais making the tough decisions." There was a knock at the door and he moved to open it for Leslie Longland.

"An interview, sir? I'm in the middle of—"

"Carry on, Marti. Leslie wants to witness that rat-eating deviant being led away in chains."

"Sir!"

"Kidding, Marti, kidding." He started guiding Leslie to the courtroom with a hand on the small of her back. "But I will say that if a dog killed a living creature in front of my kids, it wouldn't get a day in court. We are too soft on dogs in this town."

CHAPTER 18

*M*arti turned off the ignition and left the music playing. She wasn't avoiding Hank, exactly. His salsa-dance greeting was a highlight of her day. But it had been a long one, and she was tired. Tired of winter, tired of politics, tired of the mean boys at work, tired of missing her husband and tired of trying to outsmart her big puppy. It was only four more days till Oliver's course ended, but what then? More than anything else, she was tired of uncertainty.

She turned up the radio and sang along with The Eagles. "Desperado." That was a good one. Fitting. But it didn't restore the soul Mayor Bradshaw had stolen from her earlier. He'd manipulated her into a making the decision he wanted her to make. Now Angus the Scottie was on his way to the farm for misfit dogs in Brenton. Jenny Kent would not be highlighting Marti's hair anytime soon.

Angus had caused a bit of a scene when led away by one of Cliff's men. Marti was reasonably sure someone in the mayor's retinue had provoked the dog to make for good footage. Anything to make his expulsion look like a lucky break for the good people of Dog Town.

Marti changed the radio station. And changed it again. There was no music that could drown out the voice in her head shouting she was not only a fraud, but a heartless one.

At least, for now, she had Hank. He was a comfort when he wasn't being a huge pain in the butt. And he made her laugh. That was a certainty.

Grabbing her things, she got out of the car.

"Finally," someone said.

A long shadow fell across the driveway in front of her car. Someone was lurking in the shadow of the garage door. When the shadow raised a hand, Marti screamed. Not a ladylike, "you startled me" scream, but a bellow from the very bottom of her lungs.

"Oh, for God's sake, put a cork in it," the shadow said. "Or sing 'Desperado' again. I could tell you felt that one."

Cori Hogan stepped out of the shadow, holding the hood of her parka close to her face. Inside the house, Hank was barking like a savage beast.

"What are you doing here?" Marti said.

"Duh. We have a lesson scheduled."

After all they'd been through since the first lesson, Cori had shown up for a second? She was either a highly committed professional or she had another agenda. It had crossed Marti's mind many times that Cori might be behind the video and flyer. With her rabid concern for the dogs of Dorset Hills, she certainly had the motivation.

"This isn't the best time," Marti said, edging past her and up the walk. She couldn't handle a confrontation right now. It would probably be the last straw. What came after the last straw was unclear, but it surely involved tears and inarticulate ranting.

"Why? Are you exhausted from your long journey up the mayor's butt today?" Cori followed Marti up the steps. "How was the air quality in there?"

Fumbling with her keys, Marti said, "Life in the public sector is always full of hot air. I get paid to suck it up."

"And to make bad decisions and pretend you're okay with them?"

"Sometimes," Marti said. She got the key in the lock and turned. "I'm not pretending I'm okay about what happened today. I just did the job I was hired to do."

"I actually thought you were going to do the right thing. Then the mayor rode in on his hobby horse, and you crumbled."

Hank surged out the door in a frenzy. He bounced off Marti in greeting, ran over to Cori, barked and mouthed her sleeve, then ran back to Marti and did a second bounce. Marti patted him, saying, "Calm down."

"Ignore him when he's like this," Cori said, brushing past the dog and following Marti into the house. "You're encouraging his excitement. Only give him attention when he's calm."

The door closed behind Cori, with Hank on the other side. "Let him in," Marti said. "He's a runner."

Shaking her head, Cori unzipped her coat. "A runner, too?"

Marti opened the door for Hank and sighed. "He humps and he mouths—all the things I've been punishing other dogs for doing."

"Well, he hasn't killed any rats, I'm guessing." Cori told Hank to sit. Miraculously, he did. Then she told him to come, and he did that, too. Once he was in the hall, she said, "Down," and Hank collapsed promptly on the floor. His eyes were glued to her. "Okay," she said, and he jumped to his feet at exactly the right moment to receive the treat she offered. She turned to Marti and said, "Close your mouth. You're leaking mayoral flatus."

"How'd you get Hank to do all that? I didn't even know he knew how."

"He knows. He's just playing dumb to your stupid." Patting the pack looped around her waist under her open parka, Cori added, "It's all in the treats."

"I'm a walking Pez dispenser and he ignores me."

"Come," Cori said, kicking off her boots and leading the way to the kitchen. "Both of you. Marti, I'm going to show you the key to unlocking Hank's furry little heart: the hierarchy of treats."

She shrugged off her backpack and pulled out half a dozen small bags. Leaning over to examine them, Marti saw bits of cheese in one, deli meat in another, and what appeared to be chopped steak in a third.

"So bribing him is the only way to get him to do what I want?" she asked.

"You work with what you've got," Cori said. "Hank doesn't take you seriously. Until you can get him to respect you, you'll have to settle for bribes. In time, he'll start doing what you want out of habit, and your bond will improve. Then you fade out the treats."

"We tried all this," Marti said. "We even held back his food and used it as a reward. It only worked for a bit."

"Treat exhaustion," Cori said. "Kibble and liver treats are fine, but they're not going to get his attention when he's got a distraction. The bigger the distraction, the better the treat needs to be to counter it." Cori listed off all the items in the baggies. "We're going to find Hank's kryptonite."

Working through the treats one by one, Cori put Hank through his paces: sit, down, stay, shake a paw. For cheese bits, he learned to roll over in two minutes. For slices of organic wiener, he flew through the house to find Cori when she called, "Come."

"Wow. I've never seen him move that fast," Marti said. "I didn't know he was capable."

"He's motivated," Cori said. "Wieners are high value for most dogs. For Hank, clearly higher than cheese, and even steak."

"I need to carry wieners around?"

"Only if you want him to come when you call. Every time. And if you really want action, heat them gently for a few minutes to release the scent. I bet he'd return from the ends of the earth for that."

Cori tried roast chicken, deli ham and dehydrated fish on Hank, but nothing got a reaction like the wiener.

"So that's the top of his food chain?" Marti asked.

"Not done yet," Cori said. "I saved the best for last."

Reaching into her backpack, she pulled out two double sealed bags. Hank stood at her side, sucking in the smell even before she opened the first one. And when she did, he went through his full repertoire—sit, down, roll over and shake—before she even asked.

"What is it?" Marti asked. The pieces seemed too small to be worth much effort.

"Nectar of the dogs," Cori said. "Crispy bacon."

Hank was panting with eagerness, dancing around Cori and offering random commands like a robot that had shorted out.

"Well, it can't get better than that," Marti said.

"I think it can." Cori opened the last bag, and waved it gently to release the fragrance.

Hank sank to the floor as if his legs had simply given out. It was clear he had no idea what to do to achieve this reward. As he waited for Cori's cue, a long stream of saliva trailed out of his mouth and pooled on the floor.

A mere flick of her fingers and he sprang into a sit. She offered him a seemingly microscopic portion, and he licked vigorously for any remaining residue.

"Leave the fingerprints, pal." She winked at Marti. "Prosciutto. Here's a universal truth about dogs and men: they'll do anything for bacon. And the better the bacon, the higher the motivation."

Reaching for the baggie, Marti put Hank through his paces, watching the saliva trickle. Finally, she gave him a morsel. "That is powerful stuff."

"Use it wisely. There is likely nothing that will motivate that dog like a nice slice of prosciutto. So use it on do-or-die tasks only. For run of the mill exercises, I suggest combining kibble, cheese and bits of meat in a bag. His nose will be confused and he'll think he's getting the good stuff all the time."

Marti washed and dried her hands before grabbing a fresh baggie. "Here's another truth, Cori: some women will do anything for good quality prosciutto as well."

With lightening quick reflexes, Cori grabbed the bag. "Nothing in life is free for humans, either, Marti."

"Uh-oh."

Cori dangled the bag of diced prosciutto in front of Marti and said, "First, you promise to do your homework. I want you to find an enclosed area and work on the 'come' and 'down at a distance' commands. Those two can save a dog's life."

"We'll start tomorrow," Marti said.

Catching the bag from Cori, she plucked out a handful of diced meat, tilted her head back, and dropped it into her mouth. She held back one piece for Hank and was about to offer it when Cori said, "Nothing in life is free, remember?"

Marti asked Hank to roll over, delighted to see his white belly flash by. She'd had no idea he was coordinated enough to pull that off.

One by one, Marti and Hank emptied the baggies.

With each success, Marti let her guard down a little more. Finally, she asked the questions that always weighed heavily on her mind. "Where did I go wrong with Hank? How did I screw this up so badly?"

Cori hopped up on the counter, ready to pontificate. "One of the biggest problems I see is that women are simply too embarrassed and self-conscious to discipline their dogs. Especially in places like Dog Town, where judgment is high. And when a dog feels that emotion, he doesn't recognize it as embarrassment, but fear. Then he can't feel secure in your leadership. He may try to fill the gap himself—usually in a way that creates more embarrassment. And the cycle builds."

Marti covered her face with greasy hands. "That about says it."

"Is he reactive on leash?" Cori asked.

"If you mean a complete ass, barking and trying to get at other dogs, the answer is yes."

"I figured. It's a typical pattern and takes time to break. What I can tell you is that it will only really end when you stop caring what other people think. If you get over your embarrassment, you relax and can provide calm direction. The dog stops reacting to your anxiety, and can focus on following orders."

"I wish I could stop giving a damn," Marti said. "I'd have to leave town."

"I heartily recommend that," Cori said. "Move to Pemsville or Brenton. That's where all the dogs with character are landing. Hank won't stand out and you can stop being so tense."

"I always liked Brenton," Marti said.

"It's everything Dorset Hills used to be, before it got stupid," Cori said. "I don't know how you stand it."

Marti washed her hands again, scrubbing away the greasy residue. "It's like the boiled frog analogy."

"Excuse me?"

"You put a frog in a pot of tepid water and turn the burner on low. The frog is happy, thinking he's got a nice warm bath. By the time the water is really boiling, it's too late. He's already cooked."

"You're the frog?" Cori asked.

Marti offered a wry smile. "Ribbit."

Cori reached out and squeezed Marti's arm. "You're not boiled yet, little froggie. Hop out of the water while you still can."

"I'll take that under advisement."

"In the meantime, take a good look at what's really happening around town."

On the way to the front door, Hank offered Cori a very close heel in case more treats were on offer.

Cori put him in a down stay and opened the door. "Bye, buddy. Be good. Do your homework, and I'll see you soon."

"Thanks for coming tonight," Marti said. "I really appreciate it."

On the porch, Cori turned. "Back to being enemies tomorrow, I guess. Too bad, because when you're not being a judge, I like you, Marti."

CHAPTER 19

*K*inney was waiting outside the coffee shop just like they'd planned. Marti left her Jeep in the lot and climbed into the CCD-issue dog cop car, which was actually a gray Prius.

"I didn't know if you'd show," Kinney said, handing her a steaming cup of coffee.

Her warm brown eyes crinkled until they nearly disappeared into pink cheeks. She looked wholesome, Marti decided. Like a farm girl.

"Almost didn't," Marti said. "Cliff was on my case all morning. Every two seconds he was shoving something at me to sign."

"At least that kept him from bugging me." Kinney's grin was mischievous. "Oops. I guess I should be more respectful of my new boss when I'm with *his* boss."

"No worries, this is off the books," Marti said, buckling her seatbelt. "I just needed to get out of that courtroom and see what's really going on in Dorset Hills."

"Cliff gives me the easy calls right now," Kinney said, pulling out of the parking lot. "But at least he isn't riding along with me, like he initially said."

"That would mean leaving me unsupervised. Lesser of two evils." Marti grinned. "So what are we doing?"

"First, we're joining a search for a lost dog. Then I've got a list of minor nuisance complaints."

"Bring it on." Marti put on her hat and sunglasses. "This will be fun."

Kinney glanced at her sideways. "You must really hate your job."

"Well, I'm still adjusting," she said. "Just like you."

"It's a such boys' club. Complete opposite of social services."

"And health," Marti said. "I don't know how to handle people like Cliff."

Turning right onto Main Street, Kinney said, "He's not a bad guy outside of work. And Mrs. Whorley seems nice."

Marti let her shades slide down and stared over them at Kinney. "You met Cliff's wife?"

"Not met, exactly." Kinney's pink cheeks got pinker. "I just checked her out. And their golden retriever. The dog's just as perfect as he said."

"You checked out Cliff Whorley," Marti said. "The former cop."

"I wanted to see what I was getting myself into. That's what investigators do, right? It's good to know about people. So I just… checked him out. Nothing major." She gave Marti a worried look. "Am I in trouble?"

"No, I'm just surprised." Marti took a sip of coffee. Double milk, one sugar, just as she liked it. She didn't remember telling Kinney that, though. "You learned investigation in social services?"

"And through online courses. I didn't mention that at the interview because I knew Cliff would sneer. I don't have formal accreditation like the other guys."

"Wow, and you do roller derby too."

Kinney laughed. "Actually, no. That was just to get a rise out of Cliff. Worked, too."

Now Marti pushed her sunglasses up. "Your dog... Was that part true?"

"Unfortunately, yes. I lost my Kali, and if I hadn't gotten this job, I would have been in a bad way." She kept her eyes on the road as they cruised slowly past City Hall.

"I can imagine how you felt about Kali," Marti said, looking up at the clock tower. She'd heard that its broken chimes were getting repaired in the spring, also with funds from the health budget.

"Well, you have lots of time," Kinney said. "Hank's still young."

Marti choked on a sip of coffee and let it drip down her chin. "You investigated me too?"

"Well, yeah. That's what I do."

"What else did you learn?" Marti asked, patting the dribbles with a serviette.

Kinney shrugged. "That you hang out with Cori Hogan sometimes, even though she's a pain in your ass at work."

"We don't *hang out*. She's helping me train Hank."

"That makes sense. He's a pistol."

Marti breathed in through her nose and out through her mouth to the count of four.

"They call that square breathing," Kinney said. "I learned about it volunteering at the fire department. Does it really help?"

"Not enough," Marti said. "Please continue disclosing your findings."

"Nothing else worth noting, I guess. Except that your husband's staying at a hotel for some reason."

"He's on a writing retreat. That's why I have Hank."

"If you don't mind my asking... Aren't you together? You're still wearing your rings."

"He isn't."

"He was when I saw him," Kinney said. "Even though that yoga chick was giving it her best shot."

Marti fell silent, and the scene outside blurred.

"Better go back to square breathing," Kinney said. "I hope you're not upset. It's just…"

"What you do. And yes, it's good to know things about people."

Kinney took her foot off the gas to admire a golden retriever sitting beside its owner at a corner. "Did you ever wish you could go back and really appreciate what you had while you still had it?"

"Yeah. That's why I'm here today, actually."

The light turned red, and Kinney stopped the car, tracking the retriever as it crossed the street. "How so?"

"I had a job I loved, but I got so caught up that I lost perspective—on my job and my life. Coming out with you is a way to keep my eyes wide open about what's going on around me."

"Smart," Kinney said, moving forward again. "Because there's a lot going on in Dorset Hills no one seems to notice. The dog obsession blinds people to everything else."

"Governments often press too hard on a good thing."

They'd reached the outskirts of Dorset Hills, where the houses were spaced farther apart. They weren't far from the hills, which always looked softer in winter under the snow.

"There's a lot of grumbling these days," Kinney said. "The old guard doesn't appreciate what the Dog Town brand has brought to Dorset Hills. The new guard doesn't value the community spirit that was already here."

"I'm seeing that in the courtroom."

"Small backyard rebellions are pretty harmless, but if people feel threatened, they can get impulsive."

Marti pointed to a long line of people in a field. "What's going on there?"

"Search party. It's our stop."

She parked along the side of the road and got out of the car. While Marti pulled up her hood and layered on a second scarf, Kinney got directions from the organizer. They walked through the field to the far end of the line. People shouted greetings, but didn't stop moving.

"A Bichon slipped past its owner last night and took off," Kinney said.

"Last night? It must have frozen to death already."

"You'd be surprised how many lost dogs are found, even in winter. Their survival instinct kicks in."

They got into formation. People walked at arms-length apart, so that nothing would be missed. It was hard walking. The field had once been cleared, but was grown over again with small scrub bushes. Marti followed Kinney's lead and pushed bushes aside to look for the small dog.

Fluffy snow began falling lightly, and then more steadily. Marti looked up to see five women coming across the field towards them. The woman in the middle was slightly ahead but all of them walked in perfect unison, almost gliding over the snow. They looked like something out of a movie. A parka'd posse.

Kinney saw her staring and pulled down her scarf. "Rescue Mafia. Took them long enough."

Marti stared hard, picking out Bridget Linsmore from the ranks. She seen her often at the Thanksgiving rescue pageant. Pulling her hand even lower, she mumbled, "I hope Cori doesn't recognize me."

"Too late." Kinney laughed and Marti glanced over in time to see two neon flares waving at her through the snow. "But don't worry. Out here, we're all on the same side. At least till the dog's found."

The Rescue Mafia joined the end of the line and it felt like they all fell into step with Cori, who was somehow always slightly ahead.

About an hour later, someone yelled, "FOUND." The word carried up the row, on smile after smile.

Everyone turned and tramped toward the sound. Two

donkeys with shaggy coats stood with their heads hanging over a fence, looking for handouts. A man was standing beside them tucking the bichon inside his parka.

"He's okay," he called. "Must have stayed inside overnight with the donkeys."

The crowd closed in, jubilant. There was laughter and hugging, and tears as the owner, an older woman, staggered through the snow toward them.

Tears beaded and froze on Marti's eyelashes as she watched the reunion, but Kinney was tugging at her sleeve. "We've got more calls. Let's go."

The last of Marti's coffee had frozen solid in the cup when they got back to the car. "That was amazing," she said. "It's the kind of community spirit we should be celebrating in Dorset Hills instead of ratting out our neighbors."

"Agreed," Kinney said. "There's still plenty of good in this city."

Marti held her hands to the heater as they headed back towards town. "Kinney, when you 'checked me out,' did you learn anything I should be worried about?"

"Other than Hank, no. But you can't keep a secret like Hank for long around here."

"It's only a few more days till Oliver's done and we'll need to figure something out. Do you think Cliff knows?"

Kinney thought about it. "He's not much of an investigator if he doesn't. But I think it would be written all over his face, right?"

She swung into a long driveway, turned off the ignition and checked her phone.

"What's the problem here?" Marti asked.

"Possible domestic violence. Neighbor reported a loud argument and a whole lot of barking. Cops came and went and the barking continued."

A skinny man his late twenties answered the door. His eyes were red-rimmed and bloodshot.

"Hey there," Kinney said. "I'm with Canine Corrections. Just here because your dog sounds real upset."

In fact, the dog was howling from somewhere inside the house.

"Yeah," the guy said. "My girlfriend's leaving us, and I think the dog knows."

"I'm sorry to hear that." Kinney said. "I'm good with dogs. Want me to talk to him?"

The young man blinked a few times. "Talk to the dog? Sure, I guess. Why not?"

"Sounds good. This is Marti. She's training with me."

The guy stepped back so they could pass.

Inside, the house was a mess. Someone was dismembering a home and life together bit by bit. The girlfriend was sitting on the kitchen floor surrounded by pots and pans. She'd been crying, too; mascara was smudged all the way to the corners of her mouth. The dog, a huge German shepherd, sat beside her. He didn't get up when Kinney and Marti came in and introduced themselves. He never took his eyes off his mistress. After a minute or two, he threw his head back and let out a mournful howl. His mouth formed a perfect "O."

Marti's eyes welled up at the sound, and she hung back. Kinney, on the other hand, plunked herself down between the woman and the dog. "Hey, buddy," she said. "You've got yourself all worked up for nothing. This lady's never going to leave you."

The girlfriend swiped at the mascara streaks with the sleeve of her T-shirt. "I can't take him with me. I'll be staying with my parents and they're allergic."

"Then maybe you'd better sit tight for awhile," Kinney said. "You know dogs get broken hearts, too? Some of them—the smart breeds, like shepherds—never get over it. Never."

Fresh tears streamed down the young woman's face. "I can't do this."

"Can't do what?"

"Him." She jerked her thumb toward the boyfriend, who was looking forlorn just outside the kitchen. "He took a job driving a truck. He'll be away over twenty days a month. What's the point in staying together?"

"Ah. I get it. But it isn't easy finding any job these days, let alone your dream job. I was unemployed for a while and it was scary. Had to borrow money for my vet bills, you know?"

"Yeah. It's been tough for us too. I'm a landscaper, so I'm off work all winter." She set the pots one inside the other. "I don't want to be here alone."

"You wouldn't be alone," Kinney said. "You've got your main guy."

The dog had flattened himself on the floor and laid a long black nose on the woman's knee. His eyes showed white around the brown.

"His name is Whiskey."

At the sound of his name, Whiskey's ears stood up, and then flattened again instantly. The woman laughed and the ears came back to half-mast.

"You're his whole world," Kinney said. "Where would he stay if you left?"

"His mom's." The girl flicked a glance at her boyfriend. "We moved here because of her. I hate this town."

"So, I have an idea," Kinney said. "Shoot me down if you must."

The woman ran her hand over Whiskey's ears, and the boyfriend edged into the room to listen. "Okay."

"You're off work till spring. And you've got a nice pickup truck sitting outside that your boyfriend won't be using since he's driving a rig."

"And?"

"You know where it's nice this time of year?"

"Where?"

"Anyplace but Dorset Hills."

The girl laughed, and her boyfriend did too.

"Pack a few things, grab Whiskey, and hit the road. Meet up with your boyfriend in cool places. It'll be a highway romance, like people write songs about."

"I write songs," the woman said, perking up.

"Then you'd be all set." Kinney looked over her shoulder at the guy. "What do you say?"

He just nodded, and a couple of tears rolled down his face.

Meanwhile Whiskey climbed into the woman's lap and curled into an impossibly small ball for such a big dog.

"I bet Whiskey loves your music," Marti said.

The woman looked over at her boyfriend and laughed. "Whiskey whines when I sing. It hurts his ears."

"I love it, though," her boyfriend said. "When I get some money saved up, we're going to record your music."

"Okay," the woman said. "That sounds good."

He walked the last few feet, sat down on the floor and folded dog and girl into his arms.

Kinney pushed backwards and up, and then helped Marti to her feet. They left without another word and were halfway back to town before Marti finally asked, "How did you know about the music?"

"The guitar was sitting in the hall with her backpack. I knew it had to be the most important thing to her. I mean, other than the dog. She couldn't leave Whiskey, but the guy didn't know it and the dog didn't know it."

"That was incredible," Marti said, fighting tears again. "Good job."

"People back themselves into a corner sometimes and they just don't know how to get out. Usually the best thing to do is to put the dog first, and everything else falls into place. If they're lucky enough to have a dog."

"The good people usually do, right?"

"Exactly. Beyond that, you can't go wrong climbing into a truck and taking off for awhile."

Marti rolled the window down and let the cool wind dry her face. "You know where it's nice this time of year?"

"Anyplace but Dorset Hills," they said in unison, and laughed.

arti had visited Tonna's club, Beta Dogs, often over the years. In was in a large renovated auto-body shop at the end of a residential street. You could hear the barking from a block away, but the neighbors never complained. Tonna wisely offered a very steep discount for doggie day care and free coffee and chocolate to every resident on the street.

Inside, it was controlled chaos. There was a large play area where up to 30 dogs gathered for a day of supervised revelry, and smaller rooms for seniors and puppies, as well as a spa for grooming. What set Beta Dogs apart from other doggie day care facilities was the café upstairs. Marble counters and brass fixtures offered a stylish contrast to the mayhem below. Still, you knew you were among dogs by the smell of industrial detergent. It was part of the package.

The cappuccino served was one of the best in Dorset Hills, and Marti had used her previous barista experience to train the staff how to make dog bones and other cute shapes on the foam. A long, slim counter and stools along a glass wall overlooked the puppy room. Years before Hank became a reality, Marti would drive over on Saturday mornings to ogle the pups for half an hour before going into the office. She was never alone; lots of dogless people did the same.

There wasn't a seat to be had this particular Saturday morning. Tonna had sent out a mysterious invitation the day before to friends and clients. Even Marti didn't know the secret, although she had her suspicions.

Tonna rushed over when she saw Marti and hugged her. She was wearing her usual work uniform of a tank top and overalls, and her hair was in pigtails. Somehow, she still looked elegant.

"Hold your breath," she whispered. "A dog peed on me earlier. Poor old thing."

"What's going on?" Marti asked. "You look as excited as Hank when there's prosciutto in smelling distance."

"I'm going to do a big announce in a few minutes," Tonna said. "The only one more excited than me is Levi."

"Levi? Wait a second. Are you two getting serious?"

Tonna grinned. "Kind of. We're taking it to the next level."

Marti had met Levi a couple of times, but he played in a band and was on the road a lot. Now he emerged from the crowd and kissed Marti's cheek.

Levi was three inches shorter than Tonna, and about ten pounds lighter. Two dense sleeves of tattoos and a number of piercings made him look intimidating, but he was surprisingly down to earth. Since he'd met Tonna, the tongue and lip piercings had disappeared. Another few months would probably close some of the holes in his eyebrows and nose. Marti liked to think it was a sign that they were healing each other. Ink was forever, though; no one's history could be entirely erased.

"Wait till you hear the news, Marti. I am so proud of this girl," Levi said.

"This girl is nine years your senior," Tonna said, laughing. "And don't spill the beans yet."

"Get up there and do it," he said, slapping Tonna's butt. "We've got a full house."

Tonna looked around for an empty seat, and finally evicted someone. Pulling it to the middle of the room, she hopped on the chair, and nearly banged her head on the ceiling. Everyone laughed.

"I hope that doesn't mean I don't know my own limits," Tonna called out. "Because I'm about to expand. Literally."

"You're pregnant," someone shouted.

Tonna laughed. "An even bigger miracle! I'm going to expand my pack to a new facility across town. I've leased a space that won't take much renovation and I hope to open just in time for spring puppies."

When the applause and cheering died down, Tonna continued, "Levi Aron is going to help me run both places. He's apprenticing with trainer extraordinaire Cori Hogan to get his alpha on."

There was more applause, and Cori rose from a seat in the corner to raise her hands in the devil's horns. Levi did the same, and they went to stand on either side of Tonna.

"I couldn't have done this without the support of all of you. I have the best clients in the world!"

The applause swelled again, even louder.

"Plus, I need to shout out to my best friend, Marti Forrester, who's always had my back, and encouraged me to take this next step."

There were a few claps, and then the applause petered out. People turned to look for Marti in the crowd. She forced a smile, as Tonna and Levi clapped and cheered to make up for the rest.

"Congratulations, Tonna," someone shouted. "We love you."

The man next to Marti swept off his fedora and called, "Pass the hat!" Dropping in a handful of bills, he passed it to the next person, and soon it was piled high and jingling.

Tonna called out again. "I really appreciate the gesture, folks, but there's no need for a collection. All I want you to do is spread the word about Beta Dog Two if you're so inclined." The hat kept circulating, so Tonna added, "Okay, new idea: if you insist on being so generous, I'll direct the money where it's truly needed. Every cent will go to Cori Hogan's rescue work. The demand has never been greater, and I truly believe in her."

The cheer that went up was so loud the dogs started a frenzied yelping downstairs, which made everyone laugh.

Marti sipped her cappuccino, noticing that she was somehow being eased to the fringes of the crowd, although no one actually touched her. In under two weeks, she'd become a pariah, it seemed. Meanwhile, someone who'd just come up the stairs was smothered in hugs.

Jenny Kent.

Marti looked around for friendly faces and saw Ari Torrance and Mim Gardiner near the coffee bar. She'd have to cross the battlefield to get there, and it didn't make sense to try. The party wasn't about her, and it certainly wasn't about the Canine Corrections Department. The best way to support her friend was to avoid causing trouble.

"You're not leaving already," Tonna said, catching Marti's elbow. "Don't let people chase you away. You're just doing your job."

"This is your day, my friend, and a great one. I'm so proud of you."

They hugged again, and by that time the fedora had come full circle.

Pulling out her wallet, Marti grabbed some bills and pressed them into Tonna's hand. "Do with this what you will. But don't tell Cori it came from me."

Tonna grinned. "Stay, Marti. People won't say a bad word to you in my hearing."

"It's okay. I've got a big date with a handsome fella, anyway."

The grin turned wicked. "Oliver, I hope?"

"Even more handsome," Marti said. "Hank."

∾

HANK'S white-tipped tail swept back and forth as he waited for Marti to call him. His butt lifted a few inches off the ground and then he planted it again.

"Come," she called, and Hank bounded towards her through the trampled snow in the school yard behind Dorset Hills Elementary. He skidded to a stop in front of her and managed something approximating a sit. "Good boy," she said, offering him a slice of wiener from the pack she'd stowed in her pocket.

They'd run the drill 12 times, and Hank had responded perfectly 11 of them. Only when a car pulled into the parking lot had he lost his focus. He'd started to run over to it, but Marti managed to step on his leash. She guessed, from the increased velocity of wagging, that he'd hoped Oliver was in the car. Often in the past they had met here after work to give Hank a run. While the yard wasn't fully enclosed, there was only one exit, other than the parking lot. Hank had never made a break for it before, even when she didn't know about his hierarchy of treats. Now, she had bacon double-bagged in the inside pocket of her parka as insurance.

It was a beautiful, bright afternoon for January. Marti had never liked winter, but Hank was changing that. His love of snow was in direct proportion to her disgust for it. Giving him the "okay" signal, she threw a snowball for him, laughing as he cleared the ground with his leap.

Then she let him nose around for a few minutes. They'd done enough work for one day. Cori had recommended frequent short drills multiple times per day. Usually they just used the back yard, as she wouldn't risk being seen here on a school day. The last thing she wanted was an encounter with Principal Chan or Jenny Kent. If dog hearings continued in this way, she would soon be unwelcome everywhere in the town she used to love.

The school yard was filled with ghosts of happier times anyway. Last spring, she'd had a snowball fight there with Oliver. Still a puppy, Hank had run back and forth between them, full of joy. In the end, the dog had tackled Marti and knocked her into a deep drift near the swing set. Oliver had piled on top of her, too, and they'd stayed there for a while.

Resisting the urge to glance at the spot now, she looked up at the broad windows of the school. One of those classrooms had housed Hannibal the rat before his untimely demise in the jaws of Angus.

A sound between a laugh and a groan spilled from her lips in a frosty gust. Nothing was as simple as it used to be. But at least there was a warm dog to curl up with on a cold night.

"Let's go, Hank," she called, turning.

But Hank had already gone.

CHAPTER 21

"Calm down," Oliver said, as Marti sobbed into the phone. "We'll find him."

Even as she wiped her eyes with her mitten, Marti perked up at the "we." Oliver would help. He wasn't too busy collaborating with Deanna to care about his dog.

"Run it past me again," he said. "Slowly."

Taking a deep breath, she explained that she'd found some paw prints in the parking lot, but had no idea which way Hank had gone after that. She'd driven around for half an hour, but there was no sign of him. Now she was parked on the side of the road near the school.

"He's probably in someone's yard eating garbage," Oliver said. "I'm surprised no one has called me by now. My number's on his tag."

She could tell by the way his voice faded in and out that he was getting dressed. "What if he gets hit by a car?"

"It's still light. And seriously, someone would have to be driving blind to miss Hank in the street. They'd likely call in a bear sighting."

Marti giggled, then covered her mouth. It wasn't right to laugh about anything when Hank was on the loose.

"I thought you didn't want to be seen with him," Oliver said. "What were you doing in the school yard?"

"Training. Working on his recall. You know he never ran out of this yard before."

"Maybe not on your watch," Oliver said. "He did on mine."

"You never told me that!"

"If I told you half the stuff Hank did, you'd have a full head of gray hair like mine."

"He was fine when we were both here. I guess he liked his pack together."

She heard the door slam, and Oliver's breathing changed. He was outside now, jogging to his car. Maybe that was why he didn't respond to her comment. Or maybe he didn't like to be reminded of better days, because he was in a new pack now.

"Go home, Marti." There was a beep on his end as he unlocked the car. Then a slam after he got in. "Wait for Hank there. We walked that route so often he should know his way back."

"Hank is not that smart, Oliver. Smarter than I gave him credit for, but I wouldn't trust him for directions."

This time Oliver laughed. "What makes you think he's smarter now?"

"I hired a trainer. She put him through his paces and he was amazing. He knows all his commands. He just chooses not to obey."

"I don't know whether to be glad about that or depressed."

"Right? But there is hope. I've learned Hank's hierarchy of food motivation."

"The dog will chew on a dead cat, Marti. He's not exactly discriminating."

"You'd be surprised. I'll show you." She scanned the area for a big black form and the tears started to flow again. "If we get him back."

"Just put the phone down and drive home. If you find him, call me. Otherwise, I'll see you in half an hour and we'll make a plan."

Marti nodded, realized Oliver couldn't hear the nod, and said "Okay."

When she dropped her phone on the passenger seat, she smiled. There must be a shred of hope if they were going to tackle the problem of Hank together. One shred might lead to another. While they shared Hank, there was hope.

~

MARTI WAS PACING in the driveway when Oliver pulled up. There was still no sign of Hank and she started to cry again as Oliver got out of the car. "Inside," he said, grabbing her shoulder and turning her toward the house. "You're freezing."

"No," she said, resisting. "I've got to keep looking."

There was no need. Heading toward them at a gallop was a bearlike shape.

"What's that in his mouth?" Oliver asked.

Marti was more concerned about Hank's bolting into the road. "Hank, down!"

Hank continued on, oblivious to an oncoming car that slowed in plenty of time for him to catapult the last few yards and hit Oliver in the chest. Oliver fell as he did everything—gracefully. It looked more like a choreographed collapse. Hank stood with his front paws on Oliver's shoulders as he lay on the snow-covered lawn.

"Ow! Off!" His voice was strangled and Marti saw one of Hank's back paws was in Oliver's groin. She quickly grabbed the dog's collar and moved him.

Hank stood over Oliver's face, dusting him with his prize. It looked like a bunch of white feathers. And, with a sinking feeling, Marti realized it *was* a bunch of feathers—feathers that had not long ago been clucking. The way the chicken's head dangled left no hope of fresh eggs.

Oliver turned and sprang to his feet as if pulled up by invisible strings. "Drop it, Hank. Drop!"

Hank had no intention of parting with this trophy. He pranced between them, all his poodle genes on proud display. His signature left-right shake sent a few white feathers drifting over the snow.

Marti suddenly remembered the insurance in her pocket. Was it possible that bacon trumped fresh chicken on Hank's hierarchy?

Shaking her mitten onto the driveway, she reached into her coat and pulled out the stash of crisp, crumbled strips she'd broiled at 5 a.m. Opening the bag, she waved it in Hank's direction. "Hank, drop it." It was a statement, not a question.

Hank's eyes settled on the bag in her hand, and with only a few seconds of indecision, his jaws opened. The chicken dropped to the ground. "Sit." Marti picked bacon bits out of the bag and offered him one. Circling him, she got him to turn and lie down. "Watch me," she said, and Hank did, his eyes flicking from hers to the bag and back. "Stay."

Oliver grabbed the chicken by the feet. "What do I do with it?"

Marti looked up at him quickly and laughed. He looked so helpless.

"Don't laugh," he said, shaking the chicken at her. "I'm armed with a dead bird."

"Good boy, Hank," Marti cooed. "You just eat bacon while Daddy deals with the birdie."

"Fine," he said. "I'll go and… Uh-oh."

Marti followed his glance and saw Ada Galloway hurrying toward them on the opposite sidewalk. "Snow," Marti hissed at Oliver. "Bury it in the snow."

Oliver gave a swift kick at the snow crust to make a hole and dropped the chicken into it. Then he dropped a glove as an excuse to bend and move snow over the bird with his bare hands.

By the time Ada came up the drive, he was drying his hands on his pants.

"Ada," he said. "So nice to see you. You look wonderful."

Ada was wearing sweatpants and her hair was standing up all over. Marti sensed she was bristling beneath the hair, as well, but Oliver's comment seemed to soothe her agitation.

"Nice to see you, Oliver," Ada said. "Welcome back."

"Beautiful day," he said. "I think I feel spring in the air. You'll be back to work on your beautiful gardens before long."

Spring was months off, but Marti's heart melted as Oliver worked his charm to protect Hank. This time, however, it wasn't enough. Ada was too flustered to fall under his spell completely.

"I saw Hank run by my house with something in his mouth," she said.

"He gave me the slip again, unfortunately," Marti said. "Looked like he found a hat."

"With feathers?" Ada gave Marti a withering look.

"It did look like feathers," Marti said. "Are they back in style? I'm always behind the trend."

"Not very practical," Oliver commented.

Ada forged on. "It looked like the chicken itself."

"Oh, I doubt that. Where would he find a chicken?" Marti said. "It's illegal to keep them in the city. And he wasn't gone long."

Hank was nosing around the drift where Oliver buried the chicken, so Marti called him over and had him sit. Thank goodness she'd cooked the whole pound of bacon.

"What breed was this supposed chicken?" Oliver asked. "In case we happen to see it."

"Breed? It was a white hen. The usual kind." Ada squinted at him, calculating. "Based on what I could see from my window, anyway."

"Well, your house has to be fifty yards from the sidewalk," Marti said. "Hard to get a good look."

"I got a good look," Ada said. "Your dog had a white bird in his mouth."

Marti shrugged. "I just don't see how that could happen. Unless it fell off a truck or something. Or do you have other ideas?"

She thought Ada would back off, but underestimated her. "I've heard that some people keep chickens in Dorset Hills. And that those people think the City should stay out of people's backyards."

"Ada, I hear you," Marti said. "But a lot of people voted for this mayor. He swept the polls on a conservative platform. As a citizen, I may not always agree with public policy, but of course, my choices are limited professionally."

Gesturing to Hank, Ada said, "That dog's going to get you into trouble."

"No, he won't," Oliver said. "Not if I can help it."

Ada turned and started back up the street. "Very gallant of you, but you probably can't."

"Was that a threat?" Oliver muttered, when Ada was out of earshot.

"Probably." Marti opened the back door of her car and rooted around till she found a plastic bag. "Threats are thicker than snow around here right now. But Ada probably won't make good on it. I bet she has a coop in her own yard. That would explain the dead cat in her trash. I assume it showed too much interest and she poisoned it."

"The plot thickens," Oliver said. "Or sickens, in this case. Do you think Hank killed her hen?"

Marti shook her head. "I was standing right here. I'd have heard squawking."

While Marti held Hank's collar, Oliver pulled the hen out of the snow, and eased it into the bag Marti handed him. A wing protruded. "So where would he get this?" Oliver asked.

"No idea. Someone must have left a door open."

"On a cold day like this? It's beginning to sound like a setup," he said.

"That's what I'm afraid of—that someone is setting Hank up to get to me."

"Huh. That's life in the big leagues, I guess." Oliver tried to tuck the rest of the bird into the bag. "You did well," he said.

"With Ada, you mean?"

"With Hank," he said, smiling. "Very impressive. I didn't know this buffoon had it in him."

For the first time since Oliver got back, he really seemed to see her. She smiled back, hope swelling in her chest and seeming to force out the words, "Oliver, I—"

A honk cut her off.

In the street, a sleek silver sedan had pulled to the curb. The driver's window rolled down. Behind the wheel was Mayor Bradshaw.

CHAPTER 22

"*W*ell, hello, Marti," the mayor called. "I looked for you at the office."

"It's Saturday, sir." Marti stepped in front of Oliver in the hopes of concealing the chicken.

"So it is, but you used to work nonstop. Or so you told me."

"I did work a few hours from home—"

"Just kidding, Marti. Relax. I can see you have other priorities now." He stuck his arm out the window and gave a mayoral wave. "Hello, Oliver. Good to see you back, son."

"Thank you, Mayor," Oliver said. He stood very still behind Marti.

The mayor stared at Hank. "Beautiful dog. I thought you said you didn't have one. Maybe Oliver surprised you?"

"He always surprises me, Mayor," Marti said. Heat bloomed in her cheeks and she was glad Oliver was behind her. "This is Hank."

"I don't recognize the breed."

"It's a Bernedoodle, sir. A cross between a Bernese and a—"

"Never mind," he said, wincing. "I can't keep up with these designer hybrids. You know what you're getting with a purebred."

"You have a point, sir."

Hank nudged her hand for more bacon. When none was dispensed, he reared up, put his paws on her chest and slurped her face.

"Well," the mayor said. "You two have certainly hit it off quickly."

Marti pushed Hank off, muttering, "Sit." She rattled the bag of bacon, now nearly empty, and Hank's butt went down. "Did you want me, Mayor?"

The heat in her face spread, as Oliver twitched behind her. That had come out wrong.

"Yes, actually. I've come with an invitation. I'm hosting a luncheon at my home tomorrow. It's a fundraiser for service dogs, and I'd like you to attend."

"Sir, I—"

"—can't say no." He chuckled. "It's in your job description."

"My plate is so full right now that—"

"Let's try a fresh plate. The food is going to be spectacular. I'll expect you at noon, and of course Oliver and your bear hybrid will join us."

Marti took a step backwards and collided with Oliver. "I'm afraid we can't. Oliver is in a course—"

The mayor took his foot off the brakes and the car crept forward. "Princess is going to love Hank."

"Sir, I—"

The car stopped. "My dear, it's a command performance. There are people I want you to meet—people who make a big difference in Dorset Hills."

"Oliver is taking Hank to—"

"It's important that you be seen by the public as a dog lover, Marti, with all that's going on. See you and Hank at noon."

The car pulled forward and Marti dared to take a long breath. Then the car stopped, backed up, and down rolled the window again. "Oh, and wear a nice dress, Marti."

As the mayor drove off, Oliver turned and plodded across the lawn and through the gate to the backyard. Marti followed, and Hank moved back and forth between them, as if he sensed something wrong. Passing the garbage bin, Oliver continued on. Deep in the backyard, where the raccoon had attacked Hank, he dropped the chicken into the composter. Then he grabbed a couple of branches and broke them up—*snap, snap, snap*—and threw them in on top of the chicken.

Watching in silence, Marti felt hope wither again. "Oliver."

He looked toward her, no longer meeting her eyes. "You should bring out some food waste and pile it on top. Ada might go through the garbage bin, but she wouldn't likely come back this far."

Shutting the lid, he walked back the way he came, swerving to avoid brushing shoulders with her.

Again, Marti trailed after him. "Can we talk? Come inside."

He shook his head. "I'm missing a session, and you've apparently got work to do."

"My work can wait."

"Your work can never wait. Even the mayor knows that."

Marti caught up with him at the side of the house and blocked his path. "That's not fair. How about we have a real conversation for once?"

He tried to move past her, but it would have meant fighting the shrubs. "Did you really tell the mayor you don't own a dog?"

So that was it. "I sidestepped the question. He took it as a no."

"You're good at that."

"And you're good at pot shots. That's why it's hard to be honest, sometimes."

Oliver looked at her then. "People speak first and think later when they only get short slots in your schedule."

"I'm listening now."

He shook his head. "I can't believe you lied about Hank."

"I didn't lie. I just didn't offer it up."

"Well, you had another chance today, and all you said was, 'This is Hank.'"

"Just like you introduced me to Deanna," Marti shot back. "'This is Marti.' Like I was just anyone. Not even 'my friend, Marti.'"

Oliver glared at her and now his face was flushed. "See, we obviously can't talk."

"Is that what we are?" Marti persisted. "Friends?"

Finally he pushed into the shrubs to get around her and walked to the driveway. "I don't know. You tell me."

She followed him to the car. "When the mayor asked about Hank, you'd been gone for seven weeks, Oliver. With Hank. I didn't know if I owned a dog anymore, or had a husband for that matter."

He opened the door and slid behind the wheel. "I wasn't sure you'd noticed I was gone. You hardly said a word."

"I'm talking now. And you're running away again."

Closing the door, he rolled down the window. "I don't know many friends who'd take care of a dead chicken for you, Marti."

"A chicken brought home by our dog, Oliver. Not yours, not mine. Ours."

"Tell it to the mayor," he said, rolling the window up. "And wear a nice dress, okay?"

He started to back out of the driveway and Marti kicked the car. Her rubber-toed boots didn't make a sound, so she flipped him the bird too.

She was wearing mittens, so it didn't make much of a statement.

CHAPTER 23

A heap of clothes lay on top of the bed. Marti had tried more than a dozen outfits to find the right thing for the mayor's luncheon. His assistant had told her the that the media would be there, and she wanted to look good… but not too good. Besides, she needed to be able to handle Hank, which would be impossible in a nice dress and heels. In the end, she settled on a black skirt with pockets, a white top, and a black cashmere cardigan. Presentable and no more.

"We match, my friend," she said, running a brush over Hank's tuxedo coat. She attached a black leather leash to his "dress" collar. Normally he wore a martingale that tightened for better control, but she decided against it. If anyone were to grope through his thick ruff, they'd discover the device and be horrified.

They arrived exactly on time. Marti had filled both pockets and her purse with small bags of bacon. Coming armed with incentives had seemed like a good idea, but as there were a few other dogs at the event, the move backfired. Each time she met one, the dog would nose her skirt, and Hank, normally friendly in group situations, seemed overwhelmed. He stuck close to Marti as she mingled, and sat nicely at her side with infrequent bits of bacon offered discreetly.

Principal Chan came over to admire Hank, and Marti did her best to keep her shoulders relaxed and her breathing calm. Cori had told her that the leash transmitted her emotion to the dog, for good or ill. Hank wouldn't know that her tension around the school principal was no risk to him. Sure enough, the dog's eyes moved from Marti to the principal and back, and a low growl started deep in his throat.

The principal's eyes widened. "Was that a—?"

"Cough? Yes, it was." The words came not from Marti, but from Oliver, who had arrived at her side. "Poor Marti's picked up a cold, haven't you?"

Hank started a restrained happy dance, keeping all four on the floor for a change.

Taking her cue, Marti covered her mouth and coughed. "I'm sorry, Mrs. Chan," she said. "I probably shouldn't have come today. I'm infectious."

The school principal backed away quickly.

"Let's get you some water," Oliver said, tugging on Marti's arm. When they found a quiet spot in the room, he asked, "What was that about? I've never heard Hank growl at anyone before."

"He's becoming discerning," Marti said. "Principal Chan hates dogs, and I hate dog-haters. I guess Hank picked that up." Patting Hank's head, she added, "Sorry, buddy. It's politics."

Oliver collected two glasses of wine from the bar table, and came back. "You look nice," he said. "But not too nice."

"Mission accomplished. And thank you for coming."

"It's politics," he said, scanning the room. "What do you say we pay our regards to the mayor and get out of here? Having so many dogs in one place is a stupid idea."

Mayor Bradshaw beamed when he saw Marti, but the smiled faded when Oliver came up behind her. "You made it," he said, slipping an arm around Marti's shoulder. It felt like a claw.

"Let's get a shot," he said, and a photographer appeared instantly.

Marti coughed again, with conviction.

"My dear, are you ill?" he asked.

"I'm afraid so," Marti said. "We'll need to get going soon."

"Please, have a bite to eat first. I promised you spectacular food."

"Really, sir, I'm not up to it," Marti said.

"You can't say no." The mayoral claw towed her across the room to the buffet. "Plus you need to meet my Princess."

He gestured to an elegant black-and-white standard poodle who was picking her way through the crowd toward him. Her cropped tail with its little puff on the end twitched slowly from side to side as she assessed people. When Principal Chan reached out a hand, Princess ducked under it and kept moving.

"Sorry, Felicity," the mayor said. "She's so fickle."

Princess let down her guard when she got within sniffing distance of Marti. Her long nose went up and she pranced in a circle around her. Hank circled in the opposite direction, wrapping Marti in his leash.

"My dear, she likes you." He sounded delighted. "She's very selective. You should be honoured."

"Really, I think it's Hank she likes," Marti said, twirling to unspool the leash. In fact, Princess turned as Hank sniffed her backside and raised her lip ever so slightly.

"Now, now, darling," the mayor said. "He's just being friendly."

Hank manoeuvred into position to get even more friendly with Princess, and Oliver took the leash from Marti's hand. "Hank and I could use some air," he said, walking toward the patio doors. Marti tried to follow, but the mayor's hand clamped down again. Meanwhile, Princess stuck her long nose into Marti's skirt pocket. Marti tried to nudge her away, but she was persistent.

"Princess, really," the mayor said. "Leave Marti alone." He

pulled on the dog's leash and she locked her teeth on the edge of Marti's pocket. There was a tearing sound as the side seam of the skirt gave way.

"Oh no, my skirt!" She pinched the edges together as the mayor pried Princess' mouth open to release her hold.

"My apologies. I don't know what's gotten into her," he said.

Marti looked around for Oliver, hoping for help, but he had his hands full. Hank had pulled him back to the buffet table. The dog's nose was in the air, and his head swivelled from side to side. Recognizing the danger signs, Marti took a few hobbling steps toward them, clutching her skirt. On the table were several trays of beautifully arranged prosciutto slices. She recognized the red tray from Bertucci's Fine Italian Meats and knew it was too much temptation for Hank. They had to get him out of there.

Oliver gave Hank's leash a sharp yank, but it was like using a squirt gun on a fire at the moment of combustion. There was a flash of black-and-white as Hank leapt and sprawled on the loaded buffet table, like a killer whale breeching. Prosciutto disappeared into his gaping maw. As he floundered, there was a creaking noise, and the table collapsed.

Amid the clatter of breaking dishes and a few shrill screams, half a dozen dogs descended on the feast. Princess and Hank shared a tray.

Oliver seemed to be paralysed. He didn't move as Marti came running up, her torn skirt flapping. Flinging herself on Hank, she wrestled him off the floor buffet. But he wallowed over to one side to dump Marti off, and she slipped. She ended up staring at the ceiling. A broken plate dug into her back.

Finally spurred into action, Oliver leaned over, grabbed Marti's arms and yanked her to her feet. Whipping off his sport jacket, he tossed it to her. As she tied the jacket around her waist, Oliver said, "Hank, come." It wasn't so much the volume as the tone that got Hank's attention. He raised his head, still chewing.

Seeing Oliver's face, he came to his side. It wasn't a cower, exactly, but far from his usual swagger.

The mayor, meanwhile, was having even more difficulty persuading Princess to leave the booty. "Princess, leave it," he roared.

Princess grazed on, impervious.

"Let's go," Oliver said, pulling Hank with one hand, and Marti with the other.

"Wait, Marti." It was the mayor; he'd given up on Princess.

"Mayor, I'm so sorry," Marti said.

Pulling a monogrammed handkerchief out of his pocket, he wiped his brow. "I'll expect you in my office tomorrow with an issues management plan."

"WE'VE GOT to do something about this dog," Oliver said. "That was just…"

"Humiliating. I know." Marti reached for the light on the bedside table and switched it off.

They lay there in the dark, shoulders touching. At approximately the same moment, they both started laughing. It went on and on till the bed shook. Hank got up from his spot by the door and stuck his wet nose in Marti's cheek.

"Get away from me, you oaf," she said.

"Sorry," Oliver said.

"Not you. Hank. He smells like bacon."

Oliver, on the other hand, smelled amazing. Like home and history and dreams come true. She didn't want to move or even breathe too deeply in case he faded away again. But after a few minutes, the laughter built up inside and she exploded.

When the next fit passed, Oliver said, "It's good to hear you laugh like that. It feels like it's been years."

He pulled her over and she snuggled into her old nook. "Just one year, probably," she said. "Since Hank arrived."

She kept very still, afraid Oliver would push her away, but he just said, "You think he ruined everything."

"No, I think he *changed* everything. Change is usually only bad until you can see the good that came out of it."

"And now you do?"

"Now I do."

"I do, too."

Their bodies tangled in wonderfully familiar ways. Yet still Hank managed to ease himself up over the end of the bed in a stealth move, and ever so gently drape himself on top of them.

"As if we wouldn't notice that," Marti said. "It's only a hundred pounds of fur."

Oliver got out of bed to evict him. "Sorry, buddy. I intend to use up every bit of this bed tonight, and three is definitely a crowd.

CHAPTER 24

*W*hen the alarm went off on Monday morning, Marti stretched happily and rolled toward the warmth. It turned out to be coming from her canine heater, lying on his back with his paws in the air. Oliver had left the house already; the emptiness was palpable. She hoped he didn't regret their reunion, because it was the only thing that made getting up and facing this day bearable.

Reaching for her phone on the nightstand, she looked for word from him. There was nothing but a new e-mail, which she clicked automatically.

It was from DogFraudBuster. She fumbled for the light and sat up. The video attached was a short clip of Hank. He was prancing down the sidewalk with his fluffy black tail aloft, white tip waving like a flag. Dangling from his jaws was a white silkie bantam. A few minutes on Google had identified the breed of the hen now frozen in the composter.

In the video, Hank stopped dead and gave his prize a rapid left-right shake. Feathers flew up in a mini snow-shower. Then Hank pranced out the frame. He looked completely and utterly delighted.

Meanwhile, real-life Hank apparently sensed a shift in the mood. He cracked open one eye and looked at Marti. "Oh, Hank," she said. "We are in so much trouble. You've outdone yourself this time."

Hank closed his eye, readjusted, and sighed.

~

MARTI SKIPPED HALF her morning routine and got to work even earlier than usual. Nonetheless, most people were already at their desks. It was as if they knew it was going to be a big day. She forced smiles and good mornings to all and retreated to her office. In a few minutes Cliff poked his head in and offered to get her a coffee. That was when she knew something was really wrong.

There were no calls or messages from the mayor, so she prepared for the day as it was scheduled. Twenty minutes before her 10 a.m. hearing she slipped her robes over her sweater and vest, and headed into the courtroom. Normally, the chairs would still be empty, but today they were filling fast.

Taking her seat on the dais, Marti opened her file. The case was just a dog poop infraction between neighbors that got out of hand. She expected it to be simple.

Glancing up, however, she saw that the faces in the front row didn't match the case on her schedule.

"Good morning, Mr. Maxwell," she said. "I'm surprised to see you and Delilah back."

"That makes two of us," he said. "I only got the notice to appear yesterday."

"Interesting," Marti said. "Since our office is closed on Sunday."

She looked left, to the door to the CCD offices, and saw Cliff standing there. His bristly mustache was doing a little happy dance.

"Well, let's go ahead then. I didn't get any paperwork, but since I'm familiar with the particulars of Mrs. Andrews' complaint. I think we can wing it."

"Pun intended, Judge?" Mr. Maxwell said. "Because this chicken business has me clucking mad."

Marti raised a hand for silence. "I see Mrs. Andrews is also here, so I take it there's been more fence hopping. Did I make a mistake in giving Delilah a second chance?"

"No, ma'am," Mr. Maxwell said. "I haven't left her unattended for one second."

"Perhaps Mrs. Andrews can enlighten us as to why we're here, then," Marti said. "Did you catch Delilah in your yard?"

"Not personally," Noreen Andrews said, shifting uneasily in her folding chair. "Someone sent me a video of Delilah leaving my yard, your honor. I didn't lodge another complaint. I just got a notice to appear as well."

"Ah, the plot chickens," Mr. Maxwell said. "Someone's playing games with us."

"I'm sure we'll get to the bottom of it," Marti said. "This video you mentioned, Mrs. Andrews. Do you know where it came from?"

"Someone called 'DogFraudBuster,'" Mrs. Andrews said. "It's obviously a fake account."

Marti ran her hand over her gavel and took a deep breath. She was in for it now. "Please describe what you saw in this video."

"I saw Delilah walking out of my back gate. It was open, and I always lock it."

"Is there more?" Marti pressed.

Mrs. Andrews looked down at her hands, clasped in her lap. "Delilah was carrying something white and fluffy."

"Well, then," Marti said. "I'd better take a look at the video."

"Allow me," Paul Maxwell said. "Noreen was good enough to share it with me in advance."

Handing Delilah's leash to his wife, he rose from his seat and placed a tablet in front of Marti. He gave her a second and when she didn't move, he reached over and pressed play.

Marti covered her mouth just in time to turn a gasp into a cough. The video showed a black-and-white canine backside leaving someone's yard. There was a momentary glimpse of the dog in profile showing a white object in its jaws. "What's the dog carrying?"

"It's a white chicken, your honor," Paul Maxwell said.

"Are you sure about that?" she asked.

"Quite sure," he said, grinning. "If you blow it up, you'll see it's bigger than a pigeon and trailing feathers. I'm sorry to report that it's no longer of this world."

"I don't see what's so funny about a dead chicken," Mrs. Andrews said.

"You wouldn't," he said.

"Mr. Maxwell, I don't see anything funny about it either," Marti said. "I'm sorry for your loss, Noreen."

"Don't be sorry," Noreen said. "It's not *my* chicken."

"And it's not my dog," Paul said.

"It most certainly is," Noreen said.

"If I may, your honor." Paul stepped forward and cued up the video again. He pressed pause at the right moment. "Take a good look at the dog's tail, Judge Marti. It's got a tuft of white on the end." He turned to his wife. "Honey?"

Mrs. Maxwell turned Delilah around to reveal a scrawny black tail. Marti barely glanced at Delilah.

She'd know Hank's fluffy, white-tipped tail anywhere.

~

"MARTI, ARE YOU ALL RIGHT?"

Marti looked away from the mirror in the ladies' room to find Kinney Butterfield standing beside her. She hadn't even heard her come in.

"Just a bit light-headed," Marti said. "I recessed the case for an hour."

"Can I get you something to eat? A coffee?"

Marti shook her head. "I'll be fine."

"You don't look fine."

It was true. Marti saw that her face was pale and her eyes bloodshot. She looked gaunt, as if she hadn't eaten in awhile. Now that she thought about it, she probably hadn't. It seemed like a waste of time when Old Faithful was just waiting for ammunition.

Kinney, on the other hand, seemed to have bloomed since they met at the job interview. Had it been only last week?

Turning, Kinney scanned for feet in the cubicles. Then she washed her hands again. Stalling.

"What is it, Kinney?" Marti asked.

"You asked me to let you know if I heard any worrisome information, correct?"

"Yes. Tell me."

With quiet efficiency, Kinney explained that an informant had contacted the Tattle Tail hotline and shared a photo of Marti at the Beta Dog club launch party. "Apparently, you donated money to a fund earmarked to help dogs banned from Dorset Hills. Your name is listed as a 'generous contributor' on a rescue website."

"Ah. A conflict of interest," Marti said. Of all the things she expected to get nailed for, it wasn't that. "Well, I'm guilty as charged, although I didn't know the particulars of the fund. I imagine Cori Hogan put a little spin on that."

"I'm sorry, Marti," Kinney said. "If you'd prefer to keep this quiet—"

Folding a paper towel, Marti dampened it with cold water and patted her face. "Thank you, but no, Kinney. I want you to submit a report today."

"But…"

"Say I corroborated it." She started scrubbing at the mascara circles under her eyes, and then stopped. "There is something you could do for me first, though."

～

"Talk to me about chickens," Marti said, as Kinney gunned the Prius out of the CCD parking lot.

"Chickens? Care to elaborate?"

"You mentioned that the Dorset Hills Old Guard had backyard rebellions. Was that code for illegal chicken coops?"

Kinney gave Marti an admiring grin. "There's no flies on you, Judge."

"I followed a trail of feathers, some of them left by Hank." Marti filled Kinney in on the encounter with Ada two days before. "Someone is framing Hank and threatening me with disclosure. And that person was willing to sacrifice a silkie bantam to do it."

"Silkie bantam?"

"It's not your run-of-the-mill hen. Silkies have fluffy plumage, black skin and five toes. Do you know who's keeping this breed?"

Kinney shook her head. "I don't know who's keeping what in their yards. Only that there's a bit of an underground movement since the bylaw came into effect last year."

"Well, let's start with Ada Galloway then. I'm pretty sure she killed a cat to protect her morning omelet. Who knows how far she'd go?"

Kinney fought a smile. "I'm sorry, Marti. But when I signed on for this job, I never imagined I'd be policing chickens."

"Our job descriptions just get broader by the day," Marti said.

They parked in Marti's driveway, and she ran inside to change out of her robes and into jeans and a ski jacket. Then they walked over to Ada's together. Marti went to the front door and knocked, and when no one answered, Kinney nimbly scaled the back fence.

It was only a few minutes, but Marti was pacing by the time Kinney hopped back.

Kinney handed her phone to Marti. "Look familiar?"

Staring, bright-eyed, from their perch in the garage were three white hens and a rooster. They looked like the typical Leghorn variety—not the fluffy bird Hank had brought home.

"One suspect down and one to go," Marti said, and they ran back to the car.

At Noreen Andrews' house, Marti waited for Kinney to open the gate and then slipped into the yard. Kinney rapped on the wall of a small shed and a flustered clucking ensued. The door was padlocked, and Kinney pulled a set of lock cutters out of her backpack and quickly snapped it. Marti was impressed.

"After you," Kinney said, stepping back.

Marti stepped into the coop. In light of a few hanging bulbs, five hens and a rooster strutted about in deep wood chips. "Damn," Marti said.

"Wrong again?" Kinney asked. "This just clucks."

Marti snorted as they headed back to the car. Inside, she pulled up some images of silkies and showed them to Kinney. "Someone in Dorset Hills likes their chickens fancy. And if I can't figure out who today, my ass is fried."

CHAPTER 25

*T*he mayor didn't turn when Marti stepped into his office. He waved her to sit and she perched on the edge of the chair opposite his massive oak desk. Still, he kept his eyes on the computer screen without speaking.

Marti cracked first. "You wanted to see me, sir?"

Finally, he swung his chair around. "I told you to come up with a way to put things right after yesterday, Marti. That fundraiser was ruined."

"I'm sorry, sir. I tried to tell you that—"

"Your dog is a hooligan?" He rested both elbows on his desk and stared at her.

"I didn't want to bring him, but—"

He slammed both palms down, making her jump. "Why didn't you tell me about your hooligan dog before I appointed you?"

She pushed her chair back. But then she slid it forward again, just a little. "Because you never gave me a chance to speak, sir. Just like—"

"I don't have time for excuses. You took the job of a lifetime and turned it into a—"

"Dog's breakfast?"

"This is no laughing matter, Marti. The reputation of Dorset Hills—"

"Rests with me. I know."

He glared at her. "You postponed Andrews versus Maxwell. Why?"

"I needed more evidence, sir."

The mayor angled his computer monitor so that she could see it. The screen was split. On one side was a still shot of Hank coming out of Noreen Andrews' backyard with a chicken. On the other was a shot of Hank on the collapsed table at the mayor's luncheon. "Is that sufficient evidence?"

"That my dog is a hooligan? Yes."

The mayor stood and leaned across the desk. "Evidence that your dog is a chicken killer."

This time, Marti didn't quail. "Actually, no. There's no evidence he killed that chicken."

"You're denying that your dog is—"

"A chicken killer? Yes. Hank brought home a dead white chicken that Mrs. Andrews claims is not hers. In fact, she owns leghorns, and the one in the photo is a silkie bantam."

"Excuse me? A chicken is a chicken."

"There are many varieties right here in Dorset Hill, Mayor. All of them illegal, of course."

"I'm not interested in chickens."

"I wasn't either, until Hank was framed."

"Framed?" The mayor snorted. "You have an active imagination, Marti."

"Someone's been sharing anonymous videos of Hank with an intention to defame me, sir. I'm sure you can understand why—"

"What I understand is that your dog was running around town with a dead chicken. And that means we have a problem with optics. You're the Dog Court judge."

The phone rang and he picked up. "What? Where?" He spun the computer monitor around and clicked. After staring at the screen in silence for nearly a minute, he hung up, turned the screen back to Marti, and hit replay. She watched the slow-motion capture of Hank belly-flopping onto the mayor's banquet table. Princess joined him, and then the video sped up as the dogs mowed through the prosciutto like woodchippers.

There were hundreds of hits already, and the video had only been up for 15 minutes.

"This is a disaster." His voice fell to a raw whisper. "It's going to go viral, isn't it?"

"Probably, sir." Marti whispered too.

He took a deep breath and brushed his jacket with both hands. "Okay. Well. There are always setbacks and sacrifices in political life. You know what you have to do, don't you?"

"Damage control," Marti said.

"That's right. You're going to get rid of the dog and issue a public statement."

She gasped. "Get rid of Hank? What about Princess?"

He shrugged. "She's gone, too."

"Sir, you can't. You love Princess."

"I'll get over it, and so will you. We're public servants, Marti. We owe it to Dorset Hills."

Marti got out of her chair and started pacing. "Mayor, even if we gave up the dogs—"

"We'll stand up in Council tomorrow and say we did."

"—it wouldn't fix the problem. It might satisfy the newcomers, but the old guard is unhappy."

"What do you know about the old guard?"

"I am the old guard. I grew up here and I know how people think. They were all for Dog Town branding until it started to infringe on their freedom."

"That's—"

"You've got to win them back, sir. The first step is admitting we have a problem. We need to bring them into the discussion.

We need to tell them we took the Dog Town idea too far, and then promise to back off a bit."

"I'm not backing off anything. I got elected on—"

"A platform of putting the city first. That's what you'd be doing. We need to bring Dorset Hills back to its former glory and stop giving people something to laugh about."

"Stop interrupting me, Marti Forrester."

Marti fought a grin. "Sorry, Mayor."

"Our branding is working just fine. You can't argue with economics. So, no, I will not soften my vision for Dog Town."

"Then there's only one other solution, sir."

"And that is…?"

She put her hands on his desk and leaned toward him. "Chickens."

"Not with the chickens again."

"You can't stop the talk, but you can change the conversation. There's a good reason chickens were banned from Dorset Hills last year. They're noisy. They stink. They attract wildlife and vermin. You can spin the story to say Hank's done us a favor by exposing this problem. People will get caught up in ratting out their neighbors and forget about everything else."

"Hank has done us a favor, Marti," Mayor Bradshaw said, with a smile. "I needed a scapegoat, and he's the one."

Oliver paced in the living room, and Hank followed him back and forth, back and forth. "He fired you?"

"He gave me an ultimatum. Lose Hank or lose my job."

"So, you quit?"

"He gave me twenty-four hours to think about it."

He stopped and stared at her. "What exactly are you saying?"

"That I'm thinking about it."

"What is there to think about? This is our dog. You can't sacrifice him to political will."

"I won't, I'm just buying time to come up with a better solution. Can we just leave it at that?"

"I can't believe you'd even buy twenty-four seconds to think about it, let alone twenty-four hours. This is our dog, Marti."

"I put twelve years of my life into this government and I'm not just going to walk away without a fight. All I need to do is figure out who's framed me and turn this around."

"In twenty-four hours?"

"I'll think fast."

Oliver picked up the backpack he'd dropped on the living room rug and slid one strap over his shoulder. Kneeling, he hooked Hank's leash to his collar.

"Don't leave." Tears welled up in Marti's eyes and spilled over. "Help me find a solution."

"There is no solution. This town is bulls—"

"Yes, it is. At least right now. But it wasn't always that way, and it will change again."

"Maybe, but what's the cost of staying?"

"I've given a lot to Dorset Hills—too much—and I deserve better than this."

"And I deserve better than you choosing this town over me and Hank."

Tears streamed down Marti's face. "If you take my dog again, Oliver, so help me—"

"I'm not taking Hank." Oliver handed her the leash. "Own him. Own us. Or I'm gone for good."

Marti climbed up on the dais and shoved the gavel aside to make room for the files. She was wearing her robes over her parka. It was silly, but she felt like it might make her sharper. Somewhere in the pile before her was a clue. She would pick through every case, every complaint, until she found it.

The hours wore on and her confidence began to wane. She'd read close to a hundred dog-related complaints that had come in since her appointment. Then she'd reviewed the transcripts from her hearings several times. Finally, she examined the paperwork for half a dozen appeals—the majority of cases she'd heard in her two short weeks as judge.

All owners who'd lost a dog were trying to get them back. The mayor would make the decision on these appeals and reject them of course. He'd made his position quite clear. No bad dogs for Dog Town, and no average dogs, either. At this rate, Dorset Hills residents would end up dogless, while tourists still came in droves to enjoy the dog-oriented hospitality offered to strangers, but not residents.

It wasn't a place she even wanted to work anymore, she realized. Yes, she'd put her heart into this town, but times changed. And if her hometown became heartless, she should find a new place to call home. Still, she had no idea what she would be without her government job in Dorset Hills. It had defined her. But so had her integrity.

She couldn't leave without at least trying to right her wrongs. So, for each case, she'd presided over, she filled out paperwork to reverse the decision.

"No," she said. "No. No. And no to that, too."

In her notes, she said she'd never felt qualified for the job and requested that defendants at the very least get another day in court. Finally, in neat handwriting, she informed the person who inherited her files that she'd be sharing copies, as appropriate. Leslie Longland wasn't the only journalist who might be interested in a story like this.

Leaning back in her seat, she fought off a wave of nausea. The past two weeks had been the hardest of her life. She thought she'd lost Oliver forever and then got him back and nearly lost him again. She thought she'd lost Hank forever and got him back, too. And now she was going to keep both of them—and lose her hometown instead. It was crazy.

But there was no way she'd ever give Hank up, or risk his being called in front of this court. So that was that.

Taking a last look around, she left the courtroom and headed out to the car. She still had a few hours left. No point letting them go to waste.

From the car, she called Tonna. "So, I'm going looking for illegal chickens. Want to join me?"

"Marti," Tonna said, laughing. "When I said you were no fun—"

"You never said that to me."

"Must have said that to Levi, then. Anyway, you're one hell of a good time, Marti. There is no way I'd miss a midnight chicken raid in the snow."

"Good, because I need someone tall to boost me over fences and hold the light so I can film everything. I'm just going to change and collect my chicken raid gear."

Marti pulled into her driveway. The lights in the house were off, but the front door was sitting ajar. "No!" she shouted. "Enough!"

"What? What?!"

"Someone's broken into my house," she told Tonna. "And Hank is gone."

CHAPTER 26

The prints were fresh. Snow had been falling heavily since she left the courthouse, yet Hank's tracks were clear. She couldn't be far behind him.

Grabbing a flashlight from the car, she started to follow Hank's trail on foot. It had warmed up a few degrees but there was ice under the fresh snow. Before she'd reached the corner, she'd slipped twice and fallen once. She was still wearing her judicial robes and they were covered in snow.

When she turned the corner, she saw a dark shape far ahead crossing a street on a red light.

"Hank! Haaaank! Come!"

If he heard her, he didn't turn.

She ran as fast as she could in her heavy winter boots, and by the time she crossed at the green light, she'd gained on him.

"Hank, wait. Bacon, buddy. Bacon!"

Hank turned now and she shook the baggie of bacon in his direction. He paused, but it wasn't a strong enough draw.

Glancing down, Marti noticed the swathe Hank's nose had cut in the snow. In fact, there was a new arc every few feet. He was on a trail—a trail that smelled better than bacon. And as far as Marti knew, there was only one thing better than bacon to Hank.

Kneeling, she saw something Hank had missed: a bit of prosciutto sticking out of the snow.

Bait.

And only Cori knew Hank's hierarchy.

~

"Where are you?" Tonna said, when Marti answered the phone.

"Almost at the courthouse," Marti puffed. The trail of prosciutto was leading them there, she was sure of it. There was so much of it that he skipped pieces and kept running. She could only assume he hoped to find an entire aging pig hanging in the courthouse parking lot with his name on it.

"It's gotta be some sort of prank," Tonna said. "Cori is harmless."

"She's a vegan animal rights activist," Marti said.

"I'm a vegan animal rights advocate. What're you saying?"

"There's a difference between advocate and activist. Anyway, I think Cori would go pretty far to make her point about Dog Town politics."

"She wouldn't kill a chicken, obviously."

"Maybe not, but she might buy one that's already dead. As a prop."

"Marti, I'm only a few minutes away. Stop running and wait for me."

"I can't. If I stand still I might… I might lose him. And Oliver." She was crying again. It seemed like years' worth of tears were spilling over the dams.

"I understand. I spent most of my life feeling that way," Tonna said. "But take it from me, running doesn't help." She had to yell above the roar of her old van's engine. "At least slow down so you don't fall and—"

The signal dropped and Tonna was gone. Marti did slow down as she reached the courthouse. It was surely a trap of some kind and she wanted to be upright as she entered it.

She'd left here half an hour ago, but in the interim, the only light had been smashed. Shards of glass were scattered on the snow.

At the end of the parking lot was a single car, and someone was slouching against it. She directed her flashlight at the person, but the light wobbled so much she lowered it. She had seen what she most needed to see, which was Hank's hulking shape. The white plume at the end of his tail was waving. At least he was safe.

"Hank," she called. The dog moved about six feet toward her and stopped. He was at the end of a leash, and couldn't come any further. "Let him go."

The person didn't respond and she had no choice but to advance.

"You let my dog go right this instant!" Her voice was squeaky and betrayed her terror.

Finally a single word wafted back to her: "No."

It was barely more than a whisper. She couldn't tell if the word came from a man or a woman. Yet it was clear and steady and unyielding. It was no as no was meant to be said.

"Yes," she said, trying to sound equally firm. "My friends are on their way. I've called the police."

"I'm sure you can handle this alone. You're the caped crusader of Dog Town."

The voice was too deep to be Cori's. It sounded vaguely familiar and decidedly masculine. She stopped and raised the flashlight again. Once more, it shook so much she couldn't bring the person into focus. "I said, let my dog go."

"And I said no. You took my dog. Now I've got yours."

That was when everything fell into place. "Vince? Oh Vince, I'm so sorry about Guido. But you can't take my dog."

Pushing off the car, Vince Bertucci took a few steps closer.

Knowing who it was steadied her hand. She saw he was haggard. "Hank sure likes my prosciutto," he said.

The prosciutto! Of course. "You've been baiting him all along and I never realized."

"Just wanted to show you that all dogs are bad dogs in the right circumstances."

"And you catered the mayor's lunch," Marti said. "That's why Hank went nuts."

"What a freak show." He gave a hollow laugh. "That video has three hundred thousand hits already—higher than the city's population. Congratulations. Your boy's a star."

"Well, his performance cost me my job."

He shrugged. "Good. My shop's going under. And my wife moved out after you took Guido."

"Losing a dog can't break up a marriage," Marti said. She heard the doubt in her voice, and so did Vince.

"It's just another nail in my coffin."

"Don't talk like that. Your shop won't go under unless you let it. You can adapt to the changing demographics in Dog Town. The City hired a consultant who helps with that."

"I don't want to adapt. This town has lost its soul. And you're a symbol of that."

"Let me guess. You've got a chicken coop in the yard. Silkie bantams?"

"One less than I had last week."

Vince moved a few steps closer. Marti took a few steps back, although Hank was straining on his leash to get to her. He must have sensed things weren't right. Even prosciutto wasn't enough to bond him to Vince.

"Don't give up, Vince," she said. "Your meat is a legend in Dorset Hills. Why do you think the mayor got you to cater his event?"

"Old debts. And too little, too late. Anyway, it won't bring my family back. My wife won't forgive me for losing the dog and the kids are a mess."

"For what it's worth, I completed the paperwork to reverse that decision tonight."

"Again, too little, too late."

"Appeal to the mayor, personally. He obviously likes you."

"Prosciutto only takes you so far," he said. "Unless you're Hank."

Hoping the humor, however black, was promising, Marti said, "It's at the top of Hank's food chain."

Vince's lips twitched in a half-smile. "All dogs love bacon. Even poisoned bacon."

Marti dropped the flashlight and it spun around, lighting up bits of the courthouse like a strobe. Hank whined.

"Tell me you didn't poison my dog, Vince." Her voice shook, and Hank's whine escalated to a yelp. It sounded like he was in pain. Scrambling to grab the light, she directed it at Vince again. The beam bounced around crazily, and his smile was crazy, too.

"One less bad dog in Dog Town," he said. "At least your bad dog ate so much that it should be quick."

Marti sprang at Vince with her flashlight raised. She swung and connected hard enough that Vince gasped and released Hank's leash. The light slipped out of her hand and rolled a few yards across the snow. Gathering himself, Vince lunged toward her and grabbed her robes. She felt them rip as she toppled backwards over Hank and hit the snowy pavement.

It was hard to make out what happened next. There was a blur of black and white as the dog turned on Vince and the sound of thumping boots that seemed to come from every direction

"Ow!" Vince said. "He bit me."

Vince started kicking wildly and knocked Hank a few yards. The dog yelped. On her hands and knees, Marti reached out with both hands until her fingers connected with Hanks' fur. She pulled him to her so that he couldn't take another go at Vince. He'd become the killer whale again, only this time, he meant business. "Hank, stop," she said, but she lost her grip on him and fell onto her back hard enough to knock the wind out of her.

As she lay in the darkness, there was thrashing, more yelping and yelling from several people. Marti clambered to her feet and an arm circled her shoulders. She lashed back, only to hear Tonna cry out, "Easy, Marti, it's me."

Tonna shone a big flashlight with a steady hand. In the center of the beam was Vince on the ground, pinned by Oliver, Levi and Cori Hogan. Four other forms stepped back and stood waiting for Cori's cue: the Rescue Mafia. Either Tonna called them or Cori had some kind of fierce rescuer's intuition.

Hank, with both white paws on Vince's chest, was licking Oliver's face.

Dissolving into sobs, Marti said, "I'm so sorry, Oliver. He poisoned Hank."

"Tonna, get the dog," Oliver said, and she swooped in to grab Hank's leash. "I'm sure Hank is fine, Marti. If he'd been poisoned, I doubt he'd be putting up such a fight."

Oliver, Levi and Cori hoisted Vince to his feet and held his arms behind him, while Bridget Linsmore and another dark-haired woman stepped forward and snapped handcuffs over his wrists.

Marti saw that Vince was crying, too. Nonetheless, Oliver gave him a hard nudge from behind and growled, "Tell her."

"I didn't... I couldn't," Vince said. "But maybe I should have. Look what he did." Vince stuck out his leg and showed a frayed pant cuff. There were drops of what looked like blood on the snow near Vince's shoes. "I'll have your dog up on charges. And the next Dog Court judge can banish him."

"You'll have to enjoy your revenge from behind bars," Oliver said. "Assaulting a public figure isn't going to go down well. Dog Town doesn't need that kind of press."

Marti thought for a moment. It was possible the mayor would change his tune if she shared this story with him. The last thing he'd want was another incident like this going public.

Then she shook her head. No. She could say no to political games and maneuvering.

"Oliver, let Vince go," Marti said.

Her husband squinted into the flashlight's beam. "Are you kidding me?"

"He's lost his family, his business is falling apart, and he made a huge mistake. Right, Vince?"

Tears were streaming down Vince's face. "I'm sorry, Marti," he said.

"There's a counselling service," she said. "Get some help. You can get Guido back. I'm going to share my files with the media as soon as Hank's safe."

Oliver and Levi let Vince go, standing warily, lest he attack. But he just stood there, and he and Marti stared at each other through tears. Finally she said, "Listen to me, Vince. Win your family back. That's what you need to do. Turning to Cori, she said "Uncuff him."

Cori stared at Marti for a long moment before nodding silently at her friends. In a second the cuffs were gone and Vince was rubbing his wrists.

He turned and slip-slid into the darkness. Hank started to follow and Marti slammed a boot on his leash. "No. Don't you dare, Hank Forrester."

Instead, Hank picked up the ripped judge robe lying on the ground and gave the fabric a savage shake.

"There goes my career," Marti said, and everyone laughed.

Oliver gathered Marti in a hug, with Hank pushing his way joyfully in between.

When they parted, the Rescue Mafia was halfway across the parking lot, walking in step. Fresh snow had begun falling as if on cue and soon swallowed them up.

"Who were they?" Oliver asked, keeping a firm grip on Marti with his right hand, and Hank's leash with his left.

"Friends," she said. "New friends."

CHAPTER 27

"*H*ow'd it go with the mayor?" Oliver asked, when he came to pick Marti up at the courthouse the next day.

She was in her office, dropping things into a cardboard box. "He interrupted me five times and I interrupted him 10," she said. "So, I win. I quit."

Oliver closed the door behind him and hugged her. "I'm sorry it came to this, Marti. I know you loved working at Health."

She shrugged. "I got sick working on community health… Sick of living in an ivory tower. I should be getting down and dirty with my dog."

"Well, play with your dog as long as you like. I can cover the bills."

"What about screenwriting?"

"All in due course. I have to wait for the dust to settle here before I write about this stupid town."

"I just want to get as far away as possible for awhile."

"Understood." Oliver took down the awards from the wall and handed them to her. Marti examined them all, and then set them carefully in the trash can.

She looked up and saw Cliff hovering outside, and took the plaques back out.

"I guess I shouldn't leave those in his hands," she said. "The rest I don't care about."

Oliver moved over to glare at Cliff, and the mustache took itself into the courtroom.

Kinney Butterfield waited till Cliff was gone before slipping into the office. Marti introduced her to Oliver.

"I'm sorry how things played out, Marti," Kinney said. "It'll feel wrong being here without you."

Marti handed Kinney an African violet that had survived three different jobs. "Don't think that way. You're doing great work. Look what you did for that young couple."

Kinney's face melted into a smile. "That girl sent me some audios from the road. She's got a great voice, you know. And Whiskey is loving the trip."

"Hank will love it too," Marti said. "Oliver and I feel good knowing someone trustworthy is staying in the house while we're gone."

"I can't thank you enough for that," Kinney said. "It will help me get back on my feet financially. You've changed my life, Marti."

"Good to hear," Marti said. She pulled the last things out of her bottom drawer and put them in the box. Then she took one thing out the box and put it in her purse: the photo of Oliver. "Kinney, can you get rid of this stuff for me?"

"Are you sure?"

"Totally sure. Whatever I do next, I'm starting with a clean slate."

They said their goodbyes, and Oliver held Marti's hand as they walked to the car. The glass had been cleaned up and workers were installing half a dozen new lights.

"You know what I'm sorry about?" Marti said. "The mayor

promised me a bronze Bernese Mountain Dog. What will happen to it now?"

"It'll get rescued," Oliver said, smiling. "The Mafia will see to that."

"They'll need heavy equipment. Wish I could divert some funds from the clock tower repair. I'd like it to keep on ringing randomly."

"Time marches on, regardless," he said. "So let's not waste another second here."

She dragged the heels of her boots through the snow, filled with excitement and sadness in equal measure.

"Any word on Vince?" Oliver asked.

Marti shook her head. "I called the consultant and put in a good word for him. There's no reason his shop should close. He can turn it around with help. As for Guido, I think the tides will turn here at some point. Until it does, it's best for bad dogs to keep their noses out of trouble."

One bad dog had his nose pressed to a crack in the window as they reached the car.

"You'd better pack lightly for our trip," Oliver said, getting behind the wheel. "Because this oaf takes up half the cargo space."

"That's okay, I don't need much." She leaned over and kissed him, while Hank licked their ears and hair. "I've got my guys."

Oliver paused before starting the car. "There's something I've been meaning to tell you, Marti."

"Uh-oh. I don't like the sound of that."

"I lost my wedding ring. I took it off when I was helping a guy from class fix his car, and it just disappeared."

She pulled a little box out of her purse and handed it to him. He popped the lid and smiled. "Where'd you find that?"

She spared him no detail of the discovery.

"That's disgusting," he said. "I don't know if I can wear it again."

"Think of what that ring survived," she said. "It's a great metaphor for our marriage."

He lifted it to his nose. "You cleaned it, right?"

"You tell me."

Finally, he slipped it back onto his ring finger, laughing. "You are something else, Hank."

"Let's hit it, boys," Marti said.

"Where should we go?" Oliver asked.

She listened to the City Hall clock chime 10 times in the distance. It was two p.m. She'd miss that, she knew. And someday she'd be back.

"You know where it's nice this time of year?" she asked.

"Where?"

"Any place but Dorset Hills."

~

Dear Reader,

I hope you enjoyed New Year's in Dog Town with Marti and the gang.

If so, new adventures await in *Yours and Mine in Dog Town*, where Sasha Wildwood is dealing with an accidental pregnancy. Beloved pooch Tuni has been knocked up just weeks before her delayed spay operation.

Sasha sets out to find the puppy-daddy, desperately hoping it's not the big ugly bruiser owned by the big handsome jerk down the road. He's not the only one flouting Dog Town's neuter policy but he may be the most blatant about it.

Accidental puppies send the wrong message in Dog Town—a "careless owner" message. It's the type of thing that could hurt a new groomer's reputation. As Tuni's girth expands, Sasha's business shrinks. It's enough to make her question her decision to stay in this crazy town after her boyfriend broke her heart and left.

Can she set things right before her business crashes, taking her pride and life savings with it?

Sign up for my reader newsletter at **sandyrideout.com** to learn about the release of *Yours and Mine in Dog Town* and other books in the Dog Town series.

And please post a review of these books if you're enjoying the Dog Town series. Reviews make tails wag around here!

Much love,
Sandy

Thanks ... you mean the world to me!

Made in the USA
Middletown, DE
22 December 2018